DANIEL

THE HUNTER SERIES BOOK 4

KATHI S. BARTON

This is a work of fiction. Names, characters, places, and incidents are products of the author's imagination or are used fictitiously and are not to be construed as real. Any resemblance to actual events, locations, organizations, or persons, living or dead, is entirely coincidental.

World Castle Publishing, LLC
Pensacola, Florida
Copyright © Kathi S. Barton 2013
Paperback ISBN: 9781939865960
E-Book ISBN: 9781939865977
First Edition World Castle Publishing, LLC, September 15, 2013
http://www.worldcastlepublishing.com
Cover: Karen Fuller
Editor: Eric Johnston

Chapter 1

She made phone calls as she raced across town. Reilly was running for her life, or the life of her sister. The airport was holding the ticket for her. All she needed to do was show up and pay for it. She looked at her watch again. Fifty minutes. It had only been fifty minutes since the phone call and now....

Her ringing phone brought her to the present.

"Hello, this is Harlequin." She moved into traffic as she heard the person on the other end of the line talk with someone else. She hated it when people did that. "I'm hanging up if you don't answer me."

"This is Officer Nicholas. I think I spoke with you earlier about your sister?" Reilly closed her eyes and knew he was going to tell her it was too late. "She was asking me to call you and ask you if you remembered your promise."

Reilly could hear the irritation in his voice. She had to smile. Her sister could persuade anyone to do anything if she wanted it badly enough. She brushed away the tears as they fell.

"Yes. I remember. Tell her to hold on, that I'm coming." He spoke to someone else. Then she heard the loud silence at the other end. She knew he'd gone into a room and closed the door.

"Miss Harlequin, she's very agitated about something. She won't...she's in bad shape, ma'am. They don't know if she's going to make it." She heard him take a deep breath and knew that she needed to know whatever he thought he needed to soften for her.

"Officer Nicholas, I'm well aware of my sister's habits and the kind of company she keeps. I also know that it was only a matter of time before she was killed. It doesn't mean I'm not upset, but it was a foregone conclusion that someone or something was going to take her life sooner rather than later." She parked in the space for long-term parking and hailed down the shuttle with a harsh whistle. "Give it to me. Give it to me like it's a bandage you're going to tear off."

She heard him sigh heavily. "All right then. She's been shot nine times. Most of them hit her in the chest, and there is one in her head. The doc here thinks maybe she was raped, repeatedly, but can't be sure with all the other wounds. Then when whoever had done all they thought they could to her or with her, they rode through the entrance of the emergency room and rolled her out and into the doors without stopping. She's high as a kite. On what, we can't tell. Whatever it is, it's keeping her from feeling most of what is happening to her. She keeps screaming for you. Then in the next breath, she's cussing you blue. I'm sorry, but your sister has been on our list for some time."

"No doubt," she said as she stood in line to the ticket counter. She shoved her luggage, one overnight, through the slot, and took her ticket. She was then rushed to a waiting cart to take her to the other end of the airport. "I'm going to be boarding my plane in fifteen minutes. As soon as I land, I've set up a rental there. I should be there in just over an hour."

The silence made her close her eyes. She knew it was a long time. When he'd called her over an hour ago, he'd told her they'd already lost her twice. The only reason he'd agreed to call her at all was because he'd heard of her.

"She's probably not going to make it, Miss Harlequin. Like I said, she's in bad shape. I'll let her know you're on your way. It might make her...nobody can believe she's hung on this long."

She closed her phone and hopped off the cart as it still moved. She tossed money at the driver and thanked him as she raced to the open door.

Reilly was settling into her seat when she thought about her sister and what had kept her from her all these years. Drugs and money had been the straw that had broken the connection between them. In the past nearly ten years, she'd only heard from her step-sister four times. Each time it was to borrow money or to have Reilly bail her out of jail. Then, a few years ago, she'd told her she was clean. The calls and the cards had stopped after that. Meagen Harper had seemingly fallen off the planet until today.

~~~

The hospital was busy. She'd been told by the cop that

he'd meet her at the doors. There were several officers there, most of them drinking coffee or simply standing. She had known which one was Officer Nickolas the moment she'd gotten out of the rental. He was the biggest cop she'd ever seen.

She was rushed in, with him speaking as she went. Little to none of it was getting through. She was trying to focus on the fact that she was there to see her sister. When they entered the small area, she only saw the blood.

The floor had been covered in it. There were bloody towels scattered across the floor, and something resembling large clots of blood in the dark liquid. Someone had tried futilely to clean up the mess. She moved closer to where the people were standing, and when they parted to let her nearer, she had to put her hand over her mouth to keep from screaming.

Meagen's face was nearly gone on the left side. It looked as if someone had taken something to it and ground it off. Her eye socket was empty, and someone had covered where her ear should be with gauze. It didn't matter, the blood had soaked through it, and Reilly could see that it simply wasn't there. The other side of her face didn't fare much better. Her cheek was crushed, and it made her face not fit her. Her forehead had a large gash in it from ear to ear across her forehead. It had been stitched up, but still bled profusely.

The sheet over her was red, as was the pillow beneath her head. Reilly was glad when someone grabbed her, for she was sliding away.

"Steady now. She's breathing on her own, yet I'm not sure how. There is so much internal damage that she should have been...." She looked at the man and realized he was a doctor. "I'm not sure she'll wake for you, but until she says whatever it is, she won't go peacefully. Let her tell you what she needs, miss. It may not be anything more than she forgot to pick up her dry cleaning. Her body is shutting down. Do you understand what I'm telling you?

She nodded and went to her sister. "Meagen? It's me... O'Reilly. Can you hear me?"

Meagen was the only person in the world who'd called her by her first name. Her mom hadn't, and since she'd never known her father (he'd died when she was little), her stepfather called her simply Reilly, as well.

Meagen's eye opened, and she looked toward her. Reilly doubted she could see out of the blood-filled pocket, but grabbed her hand when she reached for her. Meagen's hand felt soft and sickening, and Reilly started to pull away for fear of hurting her.

"Go to where you found me when you were sixteen. Remember? Go there. I left you something. You have to take care of it." Her voice was barely above a whisper, but Reilly heard her.

"You mean the —"

"No!" she screamed. "No, don't say it. You remember. Go there now. Don't come back here or they'll —" Meagen started to cough. Copious amounts of blood poured from her mouth. Her ear began to bleed, too. "Don't come back. I'm dead. You know it, too. Take care of it. Keep...keep safe. Please...promise me. Safe."

"I will. I can't leave you, Meagen. I won't have you dying alone. I won't."

9

The smile tore through Reilly's heart. It was both endearing and sad. "I'm dead, but you have to go before… before it's too late. The letter…the letter will…."

Every machine in the room went off. Alarms and buzzers on small screens with waving lines that now were flat across it were beeping. Reilly was shoved away as a cart came in with five people seemingly attached to it. She moved back out of the curtained area and into the waiting room, sat down for a moment, and then stood. She saw the cop standing there and went to him.

"She's gone. She told me that I was never…I never meant anything to her, and she was glad that I'd wasted my money on this trip. I'm leaving."

"She wasn't in her mind, miss. She'd been in so much pain that—"

The tears were real, but the words…they were the ones they'd practiced when they were teenagers to keep her from ending up in jail with Meagen. Someone had to bring the bail money. She put up her hand to the cop to stop him before she broke down.

"You said so yourself that she was bad. I only thought that…that after all this time she'd be reasonable. I can't…I have to go. I can't take this any longer." She was nearly to the car when she realized she couldn't drive like that. She was sick to her stomach and needed something, anything to get her over this…if anything ever would…so she detoured to the vending machine in the lot and selected a cola. It was all she could make out on the buttons before she had to sit down. She drank it as she walked to the car.

Reilly had been there twice before to see Meagen. Once

was a long time ago when Reilly had only been sixteen. The next time, the following year, she'd vowed never to return. Now at twenty-two, she was back and knew this time she'd never return. She headed to the small restaurant on Tenth Avenue, to where her sister had directed her to go. Reilly couldn't imagine what the restaurant had for her, but she had made a promise.

~~~

He watched the car pull up and held his breath. An older couple got out of the new car and made their way to the doors as he watched them. He glanced down at the picture in his hand and then out the window again. Though he knew who he was looking for, he was afraid he'd miss her all the same.

Benton pulled his backpack closer to his body when a man walked by. He was naturally suspicious of everyone, but men terrified him...especially after today, especially after what he'd seen. He'd seen what those men had done to his mom, and for as long as he lived, he'd never forget her screams when they did those things to her.

Another car pulled up, and he watched. A woman got out, and he nearly stood to go to her when he realized it wasn't her. She looked pretty like the woman in the picture, but this woman was old. Not like the kid that was staring back at him in the picture, but he was thinking she'd be more like his real mom.

He knew this woman was his aunt, and he knew that on some level, she was not going to be happy that he was her nephew. His mom had told him that he was her secret and that no matter what happened to her, he was to never, ever

11

tell anyone what he knew. And Benton knew a lot.

The woman went to the counter and spoke to the waitress. When she shook her head, Benton had a feeling that he'd been wrong. He stood up and went to her as he'd been told to do and touched her sleeve. When she looked at him, he knew…knew as surely as his mom was his mom, this woman was his aunt.

"Are you O'Reilly Harlequin?" She nodded. "I have something for you from my…from someone. Would you please come sit with me, and I'll tell you?"

She went with him, and he could see that she was hurting. He was, too, but this had to be done. He was hoping she'd tell him to buzz off, making it so he'd be on his own. He knew a lot of six-year-olds that were making it on the streets, and he knew he was smarter than them. When she was asked by the waitress if she wanted something, she nodded to him.

"You know me, so the least I can do is buy you something to eat if you want it." He shook his head. He wasn't going to eat ever again. "I'll have some water and a couple pieces of toast, please."

The waitress walked away, and he and his aunt stared at each other. Benton reached into his backpack and handed her the file his mom had been updating for the past five years.

"It's supposed to tell you what to do." She nodded and opened the file. He waited, knowing that she'd get to the part he dreaded most of all. When she looked up at him sharply, he nodded. "I'm Benton Harlequin. I'm your nephew."

"According to this, you're my son. It says here that O'Reilly, not Meagen, gave birth to you." She closed the file

12

and glared. "I'm pretty sure that I'd remember giving birth at fourteen."

"She said for you to read it all before you jumped up and left. I'm hoping you just leave. That way, I can make it like every other kid on the street does. I'm pretty smart."

"Not very smart if you think you'll make it at your age." She picked up the file again after the waitress brought her the toast. "She said that you are very special to some very bad people. Why?"

"I don't know. When I was little, she taught me how to find you. Then when I was old enough to come here, she'd make me practice. I've been coming here for a long time by myself. Then I'd go home. She didn't want anyone to take me."

Aunt O'Reilly looked out the darkening window, and he could see her tears. "Do you know what happened to your mom? Did you know that someone killed her today?"

"Yes, ma'am. I was there. They didn't know it, but I was in the hidey hole." He watched the door while she continued to cry. "If you don't want me, it's okay. I can make it on my own. I got some money, money she saved up for us to run if we…she told me to take it and come here."

"I can't leave you here. I don't know what is going on, but I won't leave you here. She made me promise." She looked back at him and then took out her wallet. "Let's go, Benny. I have to get out of here before the shit hits the fan. Your mom didn't say what, but she said that you needed to be kept hidden from anyone here. Do you know anything about it?"

"No, ma'am." Not that he would share with her anyway.

"I have everything I need. Like I said, we've been practicing."

Benton followed her out, and they got into the car. He waited for her to start it, but when she laid her head back and closed her eyes, he thought maybe she'd changed her mind, and he could be free. But she turned to him.

"I'll have to drive us back. It's not far, but it's far enough. Is there anything you need? Food, anything that I can get you now before we leave?" He shook his head, and she started the car. "I might as well have bought this thing for the mileage it's going to cost me."

He watched her drive for a long while. Then she reached into her bag and pulled out an electronic tablet, telling him to watch movies on it. He followed her directions and was soon watching an old movie he and his mom used to watch. After the movie, he asked if he could get in the back and take a nap. He then crawled over the seat, curled up on the floor, and closed his eyes.

He woke a couple times. Once when he heard her talking to someone. He didn't need to raise his head to realize she was pumping gas at a station. The second time, she'd woke him to ask if he needed to use the bathroom. He did, and as soon as he came out of the dirty men's room, she was waiting. Neither of them spoke again until they were in the car.

"I think that...no one but your mom calls...*called* me O'Reilly. I use it for work, but nothing else. What are you supposed to call me, do you know?"

He had to clear his throat twice before he could speak. It was suddenly real. His mom was gone, and now he was with this woman. And even though he'd heard about her all his life, he didn't know her.

"Mom. I'm supposed to call you mom, so nobody knows." He stretched out on the seat this time. "I'm really sorry about this. I really am."

"Me too, kid. Me too."

Chapter 2

Four years later

Daniel Hunter wasn't happy. In fact, he was pretty close to being really pissed off. He'd been waiting on this woman to see him for over a month, and now that he had it all set up, she'd bailed on him. Again.

"I'm so sorry, Daniel. You must think I'm a real ninny." Not ninny, he wanted to scream at her, but more like an inconsiderate bitch. But he only smiled. "I have completely forgotten about Pogo's vet appointment. He's getting f-i-x-e-d, you know."

The dog in question looked up at him with confused eyes. He knew just how the mutt felt. But Mrs. Elisha Pressman was old, ninety-four on her last birthday, and not getting any younger, and her family wanted her to get settled before it was too late.

Too late for what he didn't know. She'd be around when

16

he was kicking up daisies. He smiled at her as she settled in his car. He'd have to get the sucker fumigated when this was done. He didn't care for little dogs in general, anyway, and this one stank.

"No problem at all, ma'am. I have some errands to run while you're inside, and by the time this is finished, I can run you back home. We can set up an appointment some other time." Over his dead body. So far, he'd been to her house four times, and every time he'd taken her somewhere, the doctor, the grocery, and once to the cemetery when she'd forgotten to put flowers on her friend's grave last month. Now the vet. Nope, he was done.

Daniel was going into the drugstore when his phone rang. He almost didn't answer it, sure it was someone he was avoiding. He'd been avoiding a lot of people lately. Especially his family. But he answered, and as soon as Kasey started talking, he wondered if she'd notice if he closed the phone on her.

"...he said it's too much for him, and the opening is in two weeks. I don't have time to find another potter between now and then. What the hell am I supposed to do?"

It took several seconds for his mind to catch up with her. Potter. Okay, no clue. Then he remembered the grand opening of the Artisan's Way Foundation. The grand opening? The place must have been a lot further along than he'd realized. Of course, having nearly the entire state involved in the thing was a way to get a project from conception to completion in just under seven months. He realized she was waiting for something.

"Can't you just go to some studio and find somebody

to fill in until you find something more permanent?" Her laughter, bitter and cold sounding, made him want to strangle her. "I'm trying here, Kasey. Cut me some slack."

"I'm sorry, but I've tried everyone I know. I don't have a clue and the guy who wanted to work with us no matter what had designed the place to take up almost all the ground floor." He didn't have a clue.

"Listen, I'm supposed to drop this woman off at her house in about an hour. Once I get rid of her, I'll come by your office. I need to talk to Royce, anyway."

"Who are you getting rid of? That Mary person? Oh, Daniel, I told you not to see her. She's bad news."

"It's Mrs. Pressman. And this is why I stay away. You guys are trying to sell me off to the first female you see." He snapped his mouth closed. He'd not meant to say that out loud. "I'm sorry, Kasey. I'm frustrated and tired."

She was quiet, and he felt worst for it. He was nearly ready to tell her again how sorry he'd been when she spoke. His heart hurt more.

"Don't worry about it. And I'm sorry about the matchmaking. I guess the rest of us are so happy we wanted to...I hear Lee crying. I have to go."

He closed his phone and his eyes. *Way to go asshole.* He walked over to the greenhouse that his family owned and saw Joey on the phone. When she hung up as he walked in the door, he knew she'd already spoken to Kasey. He started for the counter when a kid walked in front of him.

"Can I get this filled with some flowers?" The kid laid the beautiful vase on the counter and then took out some cash. "I have forty dollars to fill it this time."

"Sure. What are we filling it with, do you know?" Joey asked, and the kid shook his head. "Okay. You said this time. Have you filled this vase before?"

Joey picked up the vase and looked on the bottom. She nearly bobbled it before she set it gently on the counter again and took a step back. The kid looked at her strangely.

"Where's that other lady? The one that always helps me with this? She knows what to fill it with. I like her." Daniel wanted to laugh at Joey's expression. The kid obviously didn't care much for Joey's kind of help.

"Where did you get this vase," she asked him sharply. "This is a Harlequin vase, and it's very expensive. And Patty doesn't work here anymore. She's...she died last winter."

The kid looked at Daniel as if to say "what the hell" before he turned back to Joey. "I know what it is. I just want it filled with pretty flowers like the other lady did. She knew what to do with it and all."

His voice gave the impression that he thought Joey wasn't all there. Daniel could see her start to bristle. She had a fine temper when she was pissed off. He decided to save the kid.

"She's just trying to find out where you got the vase. Why don't you simply tell her? Then she'll take your order." He smiled, and the kid took a deep breath. He looked at Joey as he picked up the vase.

"I should get going. Mom will wonder what's taking me so long, anyway. It's just that...look, I'm sorry, but could you please just fill it with pretty flowers for me? Then take it to the hospital or somewhere and give it to somebody who doesn't have any?"

Daniel looked at Joey, then back at the kid. "You want her to fill it with flowers and give them to a stranger? Kid, that doesn't make sense. I don't know a lot about vases, but that one is probably worth five grand. And you want Joey here just to give it to someone who doesn't have any? Why?"

"I can't give her flowers anymore on her birthday. And every year that other lady helped me give them to her cause she's…'cause she died." He looked at Joey. "I can't give her the flowers, so I want you to give them to someone who can smell them and stuff." He shoved the vase and the money at her again. "I'll have my mom come in and tell you I didn't steal the vase. It's mine. I earned it."

He went out of the door quickly. Before Daniel could gather himself up to go after him, the kid was gone. Looking down both sides of the street, he shook his head. The kid was fast. He went back into the shop to find Joey gone and her helper at the register. He went to the back to find her.

"Help me look," he told her. "Patty helped this kid for some time, and I'm going to find out who he is. Then I'm calling his mother and finding out what the hell he's doing with a five thousand dollar vase to give away."

He had to leave, but he promised her he'd return to help when he took Mrs. Pressman home. On his way out the door, he stopped and ordered roses for Kasey and a very heartfelt apology note. He was sticking it with the flowers when his phone rang again.

"Mrs. Pressman just called. She said you abandoned her at the vet, and Pogo is spending the night." Jesse, his brother and partner, laughed. "I take it you didn't get her to sign the power of attorney."

He got into his car as he told him what had happened. Ten minutes later, he was in front of the vet and still talking to Jesse. His mood wasn't getting any better. "And after pissing off Kasey, I went to get some flowers, and this kid nearly runs me over with this vase that cost more than my first car. He claimed somebody died, and he sent flowers to people who didn't have any to make up for it. I call bullshit. The kid is probably some thief and will more than likely claim Joey stole it from him."

But Daniel didn't think that was true, either. The kid looked clean-cut and well mannered. He'd been frustrated yes, and a little short, but who knew why? He opened the door just as the rider was coming out of the office.

"I'll see you for dinner. Tonight. Mom said if you don't show, she's hunting you down and making you come. I don't think I'd fuck with her. She said she was tired of you ducking out all the time."

He knew he'd been, too. He just couldn't stand all the lovey-dovey shit that went on between him and his brothers and their new wives. He couldn't even hang out with Alex or Jared anymore because they, too, seemed to be trying to get him married off. He wasn't fucking getting married. But he knew he'd been away long enough. It was time to appease his mom until he could skip them again. Sighing, he told Jesse he'd be there.

After dropping off Mrs. Pressman, he went back to the shop. Joey had just figured it out when he walked in the back room. He was glad. He needed to go home and girth up before the family pounced on him.

"His name is Benny Harlequin...oh shit, you don't think

21

he's related to the old buzzard, do you?"

~~~

Reilly looked at the pot she'd just thrown and frowned. It was nice, but it didn't look like she'd thought it would. She was cocking her head to the side to get a better angle when she heard a voice at the door.

"Might as well start over. When you get that look in your eye, it means it's not what you dreamed, or what the clay told you it would be. So toss it." Benny grinned at her. "Or you can let me have it. I can make it work."

She smashed it down and cut it off the bat, then put another hunk of clay on the next bat and leaned down to center the clay on it. The "bat," or a large piece of laminated wood, served as her wheel. When she was finished throwing, she'd pull the bat up and set it on the shelves next to her before repeating the process. She'd never really understood why it was called a bat other than when the wet clay hit it when she put it together. It made the sound of a ball hitting a bat, a real wooden one.

"How was school today? Did you have any problems with that math quiz?" She had the ball centered and now leaned upright to get her sponge. "We're having pizza for dinner if you want."

"Sure." He walked around her studio, and she knew something more than his mom's birthday was bothering him. "This lady might call. There is a new person that owns the flower shop we go to, and she didn't like that I had the vase. I didn't think about checking first. I'm sorry."

Benny took the seconds. Sometimes she'd mark them with her stamp, but it didn't matter. Most of the time, they

22

ended up in one of his projects, anyway. But this time it did.

"I'll call her. What did you tell her?" He shrugged. He looked at her for a second and then shrugged again.

She finished pulling the vase up and then finished it off by putting a foot on the bottom. She made this one curved, like she did sometimes, and wiped the inside of extra water with her sponge. She stood up, leaving the vase where it was.

They were in the kitchen, putting together supper when the house phone rang. They only gave it out when they had to give a number. He and she were the only two people with their cell phone numbers, so the house phone was for everything else. She'd learned from him to be careful over the years, and she'd been working on keeping them safe any way she could...including finding people to train her how to fight dirty. But her work had to stay.

"Hello, Mrs. Harlequin. My name is Joey Hunter. I own Patty's. I think your son was in today, and I wanted to talk to you about it." Reilly didn't correct the woman in her thinking that Benny was her son or that she was married.

"He told me. I gave it to him. I picked it up at a second-hand shop a few weeks ago and told him he could have it. No harm. Did you fill it for him?" She looked over at Benny when he seemed frozen in the spot. She reached over and pulled his stiff body to hers and held him for as long as he'd let her.

"No. I will, but not...it's a second? I couldn't see a single thing wrong with it. It's one of the more beautiful pieces I've seen of his work. Do you know him?"

"No, just the same last name. That's kind of why I collect

23

them." Reilly rolled her eyes. "Well, if there's nothing else, I have supper to put together." She hung up.

They were sitting down to salads and pizza when he finally spoke. "He didn't scare me."

Reilly looked up from her bite that was nearly to her mouth. "Who? What man didn't scare you?"

Her heart was pounding. Ever since the two of them had packed up and moved to Ohio soon after she'd gone back to New Jersey, he'd shied away from people. It had only been recently that he'd let her hug him, but men still terrified him.

"There was a man at the shop when I went in. He was coming in as I was putting the vase up. He didn't touch me or nothing, but he didn't make me sweat, either."

"Anything, he didn't touch you or anything." She put her slice down and took a deep breath. "Did you hear his name? Do you think he was...I don't know looking for you?"

She still had nightmares about seeing her sister. She knew that Benny had seen her, too, had actually seen them hurting her. She couldn't imagine what he was going through with that knowledge. And even after all this time, she still had to try and not scream out in the middle of the night. She knew that he had dreams, too, but she wasn't allowed to go to him.

"No, ma'am. He didn't seem like it. He just didn't make me feel like he would hurt me." He looked down at his dinner. "He made me feel safe for some reason."

After Benny went to bed, she went back out to her studio. She didn't throw anything tonight but went into her office and sat behind her big desk. Reaching behind her in the small refrigerator, she pulled out a bottle of water and sipped it. The view from her office window nearly always calmed her, but tonight her mind was too busy.

The backpack that Benny had had with him was still in his room. Whenever she'd started to pick it up, he'd snatch it away from her and stand back. She didn't touch it often, but when she did, she always apologized. She often wondered what he had in there.

The file that her sister had given her was still in the drawer here on this desk. She'd read it over finally and had several times since. Meagen had made arrangements. She'd called them to keep her son safe. She'd hinted that Benny knew things, but after that first night, after they fled across the states, she'd never asked him again.

Picking up the folder now, she opened it to the picture he'd given her when they'd met. It was of her when she'd been sixteen. He'd told her he almost missed her because the picture had been so old. Now, while she was sure he didn't completely trust her, he did love her. And she loved him with all her heart and then some.

Chapter 3

"Want to earn some brownie points with Kasey?" Jesse came into Daniel's office the next morning and tossed a file on his desk. "I found out something about a local potter that you could persuade to do her art thingy."

The file contained a map and a few scribbled notes. Daniel looked at Jesse with a raised brow. "How is this helpful? I can't read your handwriting."

"It's that guy, Harlequin, or something. I can't remember his name. But according to the county records, an O. Harlequin bought the property next to the one we were looking at to build. Joey said it had been on the market for a while, but before I could see, that guy bought it."

Daniel stood up and pulled his jacket on. "You coming with me? I can kill two birds with one stone if you do. I need a witness to the contract we're employing for the Mason Corporation."

"Nah. I have a doctor's appointment with Joey. We get

to find out what we're having today. There's a pretty single nurse in the office if you want to come with me."

Daniel left before he had to look at the ultrasound pictures again. Or hear about the nursery. He was really getting to be a hermit. He didn't like it much, but if they would simply stop for a minute and listen. For months, he'd been telling them that he liked being single.

The drive didn't take long. He'd been by this property several times a week since he and Jesse had opened their practice. Still, he hadn't noticed the large gate or the tall fence around the property. Lucky for him, the gates were open, and he drove on in.

The house startled him. He had no idea what he'd expected, but the lovely one-story ranch hadn't been it. He pulled up in front of the house as a kid, the one from the greenhouse, came around the corner with a pair of dogs chasing after him…the kind of dogs that weren't pets so much as killers with four legs. The three of them stopped dead when Daniel waved. The dogs growled once and took off in his direction.

The dogs looked less friendly the closer they came at him. Daniel was sure they were going to tear out his throat when he heard a sharp command to heel. He would have done it too if he had a clue what the hell it meant. He looked up as O'Reilly came around the corner of the house. And she was spitting mad apparently.

"What are you doing here? And how the hell did you get in?" He didn't have a chance to answer her questions as she fired them off like a pistol. "You can get whatever you're selling out of my drive and get the fuck away from here."

"I'm Daniel Hunter of the—"

"I don't give a good fuck if you're the savior himself. I said to get the fuck out of here." She turned to go toward the house while the kid, Benny, stood there watching them both.

"I have an appointment with Mr. Harlequin, the owner of Harlequin Stoneware. I'm here to speak to him about some classes."

She turned back to him, and his heart stopped. Christ love a waddle, she was gorgeous. He watched her come toward him, and he felt the irresistible urge to whimper. A woman in a t-shirt was one of his favorite sights.

"Mom." They both looked at Benny. Mom? She was his mom. That wasn't possible…could she be the wife of the old man he'd heard about from Kasey and Joey on his way over here? Life sucked if she was. "That's the man. The one I was telling you about."

She looked…he thought she looked crestfallen. But it only lasted for a few seconds. Then it was gone. She turned back to him and glared.

"You lie. You do not have an appointment with him or anyone else that lives here. Get out." Her voice was low, but he could hear the emotion behind her words.

"How do you know?" he asked when she turned away again. "He might have made the appointment today without telling you. My brothers don't tell their wives all kinds of things." They usually got them in trouble, but that was beside the point.

Daniel didn't know why he didn't just fess up. He liked watching the way her face told every single one of her

28

thoughts. He wondered how she would look beneath him and stopped himself from that thought. He did not mess with married women, and never women with kids. Too many strings that could tie you up.

"You don't have an appointment, because, you moronic fuck-tard, I'm O'Reilly Harlequin. And I think I'd remember making an appointment."

When she turned from him this time, he watched her and Benny go inside the house. The dogs, now relaxed and about to fall asleep, ignored him. He moved to the car slowly.

She was the old man. The potter wasn't a man but a woman. A beautiful, vibrant woman with a kid. He drove down the long drive and had to wait for the gate to open to allow him out. He'd bet his last dollar that he'd never find this gate open again.

He drove down the street and started to laugh. Finally, he had to pull over, his mirth too much to go on. The one woman he might want to spend more than ten minutes with hated him passionately, and she had the one thing that he didn't want more in this world. She had a kid.

He met his brother Jesse in his office. He didn't have any idea how to tell him and was surprised and dismayed that Joey was there, too. And, of course, numbnuts had told her that he was seeing her…him. He sat down hard in the chair.

"I fucked up. I got into the compound and lied to her. And the kid. I told her I had an appoint—"

"Wait. What 'her'? And what kid? I thought you were going over to see this Harlequin person. How did you getting sidetracked with a woman get you to him?" He looked at Joey as she spoke. When she looked at her husband, Daniel knew he got it.

"Harlequin is a female, love. And she has a child, apparently. And we all know how Daniel feels about kids." Jesse walked to Joey, picked her up, and sat down again with her on his lap. "He just doesn't get how much a family can make you feel."

"I don't care. You fix this. I mean it, Daniel, you fix this, and ask her if she'll help us out with the gallery." She stood up and moved to the door. "If you don't, then I will start setting you up with every female I know."

The door slammed behind her. He winced and then turned to his brother. "Why is it that every time I screw up, somebody wants to start setting me up with women? It's not really a hardship for me, you know."

"I think, my dear brother, that they are hoping you find Mrs. Right and get married and live happily ever after. Then they can rub your nose in it." He, too, stood up and put on his jacket. "I'm going home. If I were you, I'd figure out a way to make this work. If not…well, I'd hate to be in your shoes at holiday time. Oh, and by the way, Joey and I are having a girl."

~~~

"I didn't handle that well, did I?" He didn't answer her, and she cut up some more lettuce. "I should have just told him that I wasn't the person he was looking for and let it go at that."

"Are you asking me if I agree with you, or are you trying to convince yourself that you did something wrong? I'm not really too sure how to answer that one." She glared at Benny, and he grinned back. "You should have seen your face when you came around the house. I don't think I ever saw you so mad."

She flushed. She had been mad. Not at the man, though his being in the yard had more terrified her than made her mad. It was the fact that someone had been in the yard and had left the gate open. She looked at her nephew and wondered if she should ask him if he'd left it open again.

"I didn't. I told you three times already." She ducked her head so he couldn't read the fear in her face. "Probably that opener thing you got. I told you to let me change the batteries in it. You probably left it open when you went into town today."

She hadn't left. Not all day. Other than him leaving this morning, and then coming home this afternoon, she'd been in her work area. She hadn't told him anything yet, wanting to see if…she wasn't sure, but she wasn't going to panic just yet.

"I think I'll call the electrician tomorrow and see if he'll come out and make sure. I don't want people just wandering in off the street and startling me when I'm in the middle of a pot." She also didn't want to end up dead. That would really suck. "You just make sure you close it in the morning. All right?"

They ate dinner, and then he did his homework while she worked on her accounting. She hated this part of her business more than anything in the world. But it had to be done. She was just closing down the computer when the house phone rang. She answered it with trepidation.

"Please don't hang up on me. I really would like to speak to you." She hung up on him. He was persistent, she'd give him that. When it rang a few seconds later, she almost didn't answer but did anyway.

"Listen, bucko, I said no. I don't want to speak to you, nor do I want to have anything to do with you. I've asked you nicely, and now I'm telling you, leave me the fuck alone." She nearly hung up when he didn't speak right away.

"I don't really want to speak to you so much as I'd like to murder you." She looked over at Benny and hoped he didn't hear the person at the other end. "You have something that belongs to me, and I'm going to get it. Do you remember what I did to your sister? I'm going to do much worse to you." He laughed, and the phone went dead. She gently put the phone in the cradle and stepped back. She hadn't realized Benny was speaking until he handed her the phone again.

"Please don't hurt him. I don't know what you want from me, but please don't hurt Benny." She whispered softly and nearly choked on a sob. "I don't want him hurt."

"Who threatened you?" She closed her eyes when she realized who was on the phone again. Mr. Hunter had called back. "I'm coming over there. Let me in the gate."

"No. I don't want...stay away. You...you have no right.... I'm not letting you in, and if you...if you show up, I'll have you arrested."

She nearly screamed when Benny touched her. She leaned into his small chest and let him hold her. He didn't like to be hugged, and she was going to absorb as much of it as she could while he was in the mood.

"He doesn't give up, does he?" She looked up at him, terrified he'd heard. "I wonder who he is. He seemed like he was an okay guy at the florist, but I guess he's as bad as the rest."

The man, Daniel Hunter, had said he'd come there. To do what, she wasn't all that sure. He'd sounded so concerned and worried. She shook her head.

After all this time, she still didn't trust, and now this. She got up to check the doors and windows without letting Benny realize it, and then she waited until he went to bed before she walked down to check on the gate. It was locked. Walking back up to the house, she wondered what to do.

She could change her number but wasn't sure that would help. Reilly thought changing the number would be more hassle than it would more than likely be worth. She'd just have to figure out who it was...not that she didn't have an idea, just not exactly why he thought she had something of his. She had figured long ago it was Benny and that maybe Benny was his son.

Her sister had been dead for nearly four years now. She and Benny had driven to her little apartment, and he'd hidden away during the day while she worked in her studio. She'd been less cautious then. And it wasn't until she received her sister's things that she realized she might have led them, whoever her sister was telling her about, right to her nephew.

The house was quiet when she went inside. She made sure it was locked up and then walked to the studio. She could lose herself in there and decided to work on the kiln she was building until she couldn't think anymore. The backhoe sat in the side-yard, waiting to go back into the barn. She smiled when she thought of all the things she could do now that she couldn't when she started this…building an outside kiln being one of them.

She had wanted to do this for some time…build a kiln right into the hillside and use most of nature to make it work. She would be able to get a lot more pottery in this one than her other kilns, and she would be able to fire it using wood. She was putting some of the kiln bricks inside it when she thought of the man from that day.

He was gorgeous. She wondered if he was as large as he looked under his suit coat and tisked herself for thinking of such things. She had a kid to raise, not play around with a rich guy who had the manners of a…well, she wasn't sure what sort of manners he had, but she'd bet his mother was a poor example. Reilly thought maybe if she ever had the chance to meet her, she'd have to smack her. It was nearly sunrise when she entered the house. She went to her room and showered, then started breakfast for Benny. He'd like that.

Chapter 4

Doyle was in his office when Daniel went to find him the next morning. He was a huge man, and he seemed to be fitting in well with the company. One of the things he'd wanted to do when he'd signed on was being able to run the security team as he saw fit. After the help he'd given them before, Royce and all of them had agreed.

"I need your help with something. It's about a woman. And her kid, she has a kid." Daniel tried to calm himself and couldn't. The woman had sounded terrified, and he couldn't do a damned thing about it. "Her name is O'Reilly Harlequin, and she lives at…. Why aren't you writing this down?"

He'd driven by her house last night and stood at the gate. He hadn't touched it, but stood there, listening to the hum of the electricity running through it. Then he'd driven by again this morning, wondering if she ever left the compound. He hadn't seen anyone either time.

"Don't need to. Her name is O'Reilly Harlequin, the only child of Olivia and Reilly Harlequin. The dad died when she was a baby, hit, and run that never turned up any arrests. Her mom remarried when O'Reilly was five to a man who had a daughter already. Her name was Meagen Harper. She was a class act, too."

"Was? Her sister is dead?" Doyle nodded. "Why do you know so much about her? Is she in trouble?"

He reached behind him and unlocked the bottom drawer to his cabinet. He laid a file in front of him and looked at him. "It's not pretty, not all of it. I'll give it to you like we figured it out, all right?"

Daniel nodded, sure that this was going to be horrible. He looked at the newspaper clipping that showed a young girl and a large vase. He couldn't make out the design but thought it was pretty enough.

"O'Reilly was twelve when she made that. There was this contest in her hometown that was sponsoring an essay contest, some big corporation that was trying to make a community impact. Winner won a trip to Paris to study art for a year. The essay was to be about the earth."

He looked at the picture again in the clipping and took the better photo when Doyle handed it to him. His breath caught. The design on the vase was stunning. At the center of the piece was a large tree. The tree was bare of anything other than large branches. There was a single leaf on the topmost branches that seemed to strain out. Something was written at the base of the tree. Daniel looked up at Doyle when he spoke them.

"*All that we have, all that we will ever be, is in our nature.*

Whether it be in ourselves or in that which surrounds us."

"She won."

Doyle shook his head and laughed. "No, she didn't win the contest, but she did win the hearts of those who were at the park that day." He handed him another picture. "About a week after she was disqualified, a big news dump happened. From all over the world, news vans showed up to see what they'd been asked to come and witness. See, the step-daddy thought they'd done an injustice to his new daughter and was going to prove them all wrong. They'd called her a cheat."

"On what grounds? Couldn't they have figured it out that she didn't write it?"

Doyle laughed again and put a DVD in his computer. "O'Reilly didn't just write the poem, she threw the vase and designed the tree. She was accused of being a fraud, as well as cheating. They objected to the 'paper' she'd used, and then when that didn't fly, they said she was saying someone else's work was hers. The media blitz was to prove she did it all."

The video started out with a picture of a potter's wheel. He'd not had the occasion to use one, but he'd seen them when he'd been in law school. When a little girl walked up to it and sat behind it, it took him several seconds to realize it was the woman he'd seen.

Daniel watched in stunned silence as she starting pulling the pot. He couldn't believe it when she had to stand up to finish the sides. And he continued to watch when she formed it with her hands, curving out the sides to make the shape softer, using only a sponge and her hands. She finished it and stood. He held his breath when she walked in front of it. He could see flashes going off and knew she was getting her picture taken with it. But she wasn't finished.

She walked over to a large easel and pulled a sheet of paper about four foot square off a pad. She clipped it to the easel with cardboard as its board. She picked up a pencil and looked back at the camera.

"I don't know what to draw. Does anyone have a suggestion?" There were several shouts from the crowd, and when the camera panned around, Daniel got his first glimpse of Doyle. The man flushed and told him to pay attention.

When the younger O'Reilly turned back to the paper, he watched her hand slide effortlessly over the sheet. Even after only a few minutes, he could see the picture emerging. She was drawing a woman standing next to a cameraman. Both he and Doyle watched as she drew them over the large sheet until she turned back around. The camera was moved around to the point of making him sick before it settled on a cameraman and his anchor. It looked as if she'd drawn them perfectly. Even the microphone in her hand was nearly perfect.

"Mother fuck. She's that good." He looked at Doyle. "Please tell me she won, after all. Someone that talented should be teaching in Paris, not learning."

"She didn't win. But...." Doyle held up his hand when Daniel started to speak. "But she did get to go to Paris the following year. The community that the company was trying so hard to win over rallied behind the girl and put them out of business."

Daniel was thrilled. He smiled, thinking about her getting to study there and doing it because she had truly won. He looked at the next picture.

"Her mom and step-father were killed while she was away. She didn't find out until they were both buried. Her sister, Meagen, was driving when someone went left of the center and took them all out. Figured that the girl changed her life because of that night. Because the sister, Meagen, became a first-class trouble maker afterward."

Daniel nodded. He'd seen firsthand what the death as tragic as the one in the picture could do to someone. He took the next pictures and felt his belly lurch. These pictures showed an older woman, perhaps in her late twenties, lying in what appeared to be a bed of blood.

"Then one night, about ten years later, the police called O'Reilly to tell her that her sister was hurt and that she was asking for her. That's the way Meagen ended up. We took pictures of everything when we finally got word from the locals. Good thing too, 'cause of what happened later. O'Reilly had already come and gone by the time I got there, having come to her sister's deathbed and been told that she wasn't worth anything and that Meagen hated her. Or so O'Reilly told the cop before she left."

"You don't think that's what happened. You think something else was said, and what? She knows who her killer was?" Doyle shook his head. "Then what? What has you remember a case this old and keep files on it?"

He put another picture in his hand. "That man. His name is Humberto Carver. He's who we've been looking for, both then and now. There's a file on his known activities dating from before O'Reilly was born."

His rap sheet was as long as two of his arms and still some. Drugs, theft, embezzlement, attempted murder, homicide, assault, rape…he looked up at Doyle.

"But no convictions. Why?" Daniel looked over the papers, not really expecting Doyle to answer. Then he saw a name he'd heard. He looked back at the former agent. "Meagen Harper was one of his?"

"She wasn't just one of his runners as it says there, but she, for all we could find, was his mistress, too. That is up until about the time of her death. She hooked up with him about the time little O'Reilly was headed off to Paris."

He handed him the last thing in the file. It was a birth certificate. He looked it over and frowned before handing it back. "I've met the kid. He seems okay. What does her son have to do with all this other shit, and why is he a part of your file?"

"Look at the date. The date of the kid's birth. I don't know much about kids and babies, but I know enough to know that a woman in Paris can't have a baby in North Dakota, and I'm thinking she was a mite young to be having him."

The kid was going to be twelve in a few weeks, and he'd said that O'Reilly had gone to Paris around the age of thirteen. The boy wasn't hers.

"Whose is he? The sister?"

Doyle shrugged. "Maybe."

"The boy calls her 'Mom.' Benny, she called him Benny." Daniel started pacing. "You think she picked up the boy while she was there, don't you? When she went to see her dying sister, she picked up the kid and brought him back with her."

"Meagen delivered him, that's all we know for sure. She'd had a baby prior to her death, but there was no record. When we went back to the hospital, they didn't know any different, so we figured she'd given birth and claimed to be her sister. She might have known then her life wasn't going to be long for this world."

"I don't think it's over, either." He sat down and told him about the phone call and the way her voice sounded. "I think he or someone had called her just before I did the second time. From what she begged me not to do, I think he threatened her and the kid. She begged me...*him*...not to hurt the boy."

"That's not good. Not good at all. The little potter has no idea what she's up against, and if Carver finds her, she's as good as dead." Doyle picked up his phone, but before he dialed, he looked at Daniel. "Can you get to her? Talk to her? She's going to need to have protection."

"I'll try. I don't know how much help I can be, but I'll certainly try."

~~~

Reilly drove to the end of the drive and saw a car parked across the road. She reached blindly for the gun lying on the seat next to her as the door opened. When Mr. Hunter stepped out of his huge black SUV, she nearly wept with relief. Then she got pissed.

Getting out of her car without hiding the fact that she was armed, she went to the gate and punched in the code. It would open for her now and lock up immediately after she passed through the gates. If someone touched the gates or tried to climb over it, she'd be in trouble. There was enough voltage running through them to power a small city.

"I'd like to speak to you. I know that you don't have any reason to like me, but—"

"I don't like you. You're a liar and a pushy man. I know I shouldn't have spoken to you like that yesterday, but you came at a bad time, and I was...nervous because I didn't know you."

"Did it have anything to do with another phone call? The one where you were threatened?" She turned to him, suddenly terrified. She looked up and down the road to see if anyone was coming. "I can help you."

She laughed. "Sure, you can. Tell me, Mr. Hunter, what is it you think you can help me with? My fashion sense? You do have a great deal of it all your own. I don't know anyone else that wears a three-piece suit on the weekend. How about my finances? I have more money than I can spend and, as I read last night, so do you. Could it be that you think I need your legal advice? No, I have all that and more than I need now."

"I know about your son. I know he's not yours."

The world tilted around her. She didn't know how she ended up on her passenger seat, but suddenly she was there, and he was telling her to breathe. How she was supposed to draw a breath again was beyond her. And she knew that there was no reason for her to pretend that she didn't know what he was talking about. She had already given that away.

"I'd like to get up now, please." He lifted her chin up and peered into her eyes, intently. "I'm fine. Please, let me go."

"I need to speak to you. I want to help you." He was the last person she wanted help from. "Please, O'Reilly, let's talk." He let her go but didn't move back.

"No one calls me that. It's just Reilly." She pushed him back, marveling for a few seconds at the hardness of his chest. "I don't want to speak to you. I don't know what you think you know, but Benny is my son."

She walked around her car and got in and slammed the door before he could grab for it, sad that she'd missed his fingers. After she started the motor, she started to pull forward when she remembered the fence. She rolled down her window and gave him a warning.

"The gate is armed. If you're not on the other side when I go out, you'll be here for a while. The fence is electrified." She nodded to the power signs hanging low on the fences around her home. "I would really hate to have to peel you off it when I get back."

"This isn't over, O'Reilly. I'm a very persistent man."

"Good for you. And it's Reilly, and I'm a fucking bitch."

She drove around for nearly an hour before she remembered where she'd been going. She was suddenly glad she'd been thinking of picking up her mail at the post office first, then running some errands, or she'd be late for lunch with her agent. She pulled in front of the restaurant fifteen minutes early.

She wondered how he'd found out. She'd been nearly to the point of relaxing for the first time since the frantic call from the Florida police when she got the phone call from the stranger. Stranger, she laughed to herself. She had pretty much figured out who he was a couple of years ago. Humberto Carver had been her sister's on-again, off-again lover for years. And if that wasn't telling, it was the diary she'd found in her things.

It had been stitched up in a coat. She didn't know how anyone had missed it, but then the police had said her things were boxed up when they got there. They'd only found her phone number to call because the boxes had her address and phone number on them. She wondered if her sister had known she was going to get killed that night. She'd never asked Benny. He didn't even talk about the night she'd died.

She knew he had nightmares. She could hear him scream out a few times a month. When he'd first come to her, she'd gone to him nightly to comfort him or whatever he needed. But he'd ask her to leave him alone. He didn't want her to coddle him. She didn't tell him it was more for her than him but respected his wishes. What did she know about things back then?

She got out of her car. She knew plenty now. As she headed out to have lunch with her friend, she thought about her life now and how different it was back then.

She'd been taking defense classes. And she didn't take those "woo, I'm going to spray you with something, then run like hell" classes, either. She was trained by an ex-Navy Seal. He had beaten her up pretty good those first couple of months. She could also shoot a gun and had her permit to carry. One thing she was not going to be was a victim.

"Do you ever spend any of your money on clothes?" She looked down at her jeans and t-shirt before smiling at Rachel. "You look like a hobo. He probably dresses better."

Rachel Fletcher looked like she always did—a fashion plate. Reilly thought Mr. Hunter and Rachel would have fun on a shopping spree together. The man did, however, look very good in a suit, she thought with a grin.

"I have lots of clothes. Most of them have holes in them. Sometimes I get a piece of pottery too close to me when it's still hot. I did wear my best out today for you." She danced around for her benefit. "See, no holes."

"You are by far the most annoying client I have," Rachel said with a great deal of sarcasm. "I ordered you that nasty crap you drink. How on earth anyone drinks tea without sugar is beyond me. I'm, of course, having a Bloody Mary. We're celebrating."

The waiter came over and sat their drinks in front of them. Reilly waited until he was gone before she looked at Rachel to ask her about the celebrating. She had a strange look on her face.

"What?" Reilly turned around and saw Mr. Hunter coming toward her. "Fuck. He just doesn't give up, does he?"

"You know him? Well, that makes this easier." Reilly had a strange feeling she wasn't going to be celebrating like her agent thought she might. "Reilly Harlequin, I'd like you to meet the man who's just commissioned you to make a premier piece for his new lobby, Daniel Hunter."

Chapter 5

Daniel could see that she was furious and smiled to himself. He had a feeling that getting one over on this woman wasn't easy. He'd meant to tell her this morning when she'd left him, but she'd been so pale when he mentioned her son that he'd forgotten. Kissing her hand instead of shaking it, he laughed when she jerked it away from him.

"I don't want to work with you," she whispered furiously. "What is this, a joke? I don't think it's funny if it is."

He smiled at her and pulled out her chair. When she stood glaring at him for several seconds, he thought she was going to simply leave. It wasn't until Ms. Fletcher spoke that she finally sat down.

"Reilly, people are beginning to stare. Please sit, and we'll work this out. I'm not sure what it is to work out, but staring each other down in a public restaurant isn't going to help. Sit down."

Daniel held her chair until O'Reilly sat. He just knew that he was going to pay for this later and was looking forward to it. He moved to the other chair and sat down after unbuttoning his jacket, which he'd meant to leave in the car but had forgotten when he had realized how late it was. He didn't want to give her any more ammo.

"Mr. Hunter wants you to do a piece for his lobby of his new building. He said that—"

"No." Rachel flushed when Reilly cut her off. "I don't like him, and I certainly don't want to make anything for him."

"You might want to listen to the details, O'Reilly, before you decide," he said. "If you help me out on this project, I'll donate the amount you charge me to the Foundation of Art that my family is trying to get up and running." He leaned back in his chair and thought he had her.

"I'll simply donate the money, not work for you, and I'll be a happy person." She glared again before looking at Rachel. "You said you have some papers for me to sign concerning the last order. I have it done, by the way."

"You could donate your monies and mine. What if something like this could benefit Benny? Would you do it then?" He looked over at Rachel when she started laughing. "What is it?"

"What kind of foundation is your family running that a dog could come and learn at? Or is that stupid mutt simply walking through paint, then over a paper? I saw that somewhere on television once, where an elephant or something did that to raise money."

Daniel looked over at O'Reilly with a question on the

tip of his tongue when he saw her face. Panic, terror, and pleading were there. He looked over at Rachel again before looking at O'Reilly. She didn't know…no idea that O'Reilly had a child and that he was living with her.

He leaned back again and picked up his menu. He didn't have a clue what it said, his mind whirling around the fact that he had information he could hold against her. And when he glanced at her again, he could see that she knew it. This might be fun enough to get from her what he wanted and maybe a few hours of her time.

The waiter took their order, and still, his mind wasn't grasping why she'd be keeping her son a secret. He kept coming back to the idea that she was hiding him from someone, and the only name he could think of was Carver. When their menus were gone, he looked over at her again.

"I need your help. I think you want to help me out, so I'm going to assume that you've changed your mind. Yes?" She hissed her agreement. He liked this. "And the fact that I need to get on my sister-in-law's good side is only going to take a few hours of your time for a few weeks. Is that, too, agreeable to you?"

She leaned over, and he saw that her napkin had fallen. Before she touched it, she reached out to his leg, and he felt his cock leap. A scant second later, it was all he could do not to stand and scream like a little girl. She'd pinched him, hard, in the thigh. He knew as surely as he was sitting there, he'd have a bruise tomorrow.

"I'll help you. I don't like you any more than…hell, I think I hate you more than before, but you'll have what you want." He could almost hear the ", but you'll pay dearly for it later." "What kind of piece do you want in your building, Mr. Hunter?"

"It's Daniel. If we're going to be working together, we should at least use our first names, don't you think?" He smiled because he knew she was going to call him "Mr. Hunter" even when he was making love to her. He shifted on his seat and continued. "The lobby is…why don't we ride over there, and I can show you?"

"I'm sorry I can't go with you." Daniel turned to Ms. Fletcher, completely forgetting she was there still. "Reilly, just sign off on this order, and I'll make arrangements to have it picked up. Also, I got the shipment for the next show. I've not opened them yet, but I'm sure they're beautiful."

Lunch was cleared away, and O'Reilly signed off on several of what looked to Daniel like contracts. He was impressed that she read them over completely, even not signing one because of some verbiage she didn't understand. He nearly offered his help on it, but her glare had him keeping quiet. This woman was hot.

In the parking lot, the agent left, and Daniel offered to take her in his car. She, of course, refused, and he simply slipped into her car while she was getting in.

"What the hell are you doing?" she sputtered. "I didn't want to ride with you. What on earth makes you think I want you to ride with me? Get out."

"I can show you how to get there. And there is a gas crisis. Just make a left onto Hamilton, and I'll show you where to go." He put on his seatbelt, sure that she was going to drive like a maniac or toss him out while she was driving. "The lobby looks plain, and I don't have the artist flair to make it look professional."

She didn't speak during the entire twenty-minute drive. He kept up a flow of information. How long they'd been in the building, the colors that had been installed. He'd even gone on to talk about the feelings he got when he first walked in.

"It has a great many windows in the front. They bring all the light we need in during the day, so I'd like to have the piece you make for us to be lit at night. Jesse, my brother, and I have a big practice, plus we take care of the business for our family. Who is your lawyer?"

"I am. What do you want to spend on this piece?" she finally asked when they pulled into his lot. "Knowing will give me a better understanding of what you want to do."

Daniel honestly had no clue. He knew that she was very good and in very high demand, as he had read about her before he'd had the meeting. Of course, even the Internet had her gender incorrect. It never really said she was a male, but it didn't say she was a young woman either. And there was never any mention of what she looked like.

Her dark hair was always pulled back and up from her face in some sort of ponytail or braid. He wondered if it was curly or straight because there never seemed to be a strand of it hanging loose. Dark brows slashed over large expressive eyes that he would swear were the deepest shade of blue he'd ever seen. Daniel closed his eyes when she brushed past him, her scent of something erotic and female made him think of silky sheets crumbled on the floor and sweaty bodies lax in the aftermath of fantastic sex. Giving himself a mental shake, he walked to where she stood.

"It's plain, isn't it?" She walked away from him after asking, and he was pretty sure she hadn't known she'd said it out loud. "There is a great deal of room. We can go out if you'd like, or I can make you a piece that is tall and has a plant base around it. Something that can be sat on when they enter or view. It's up to you."

He could see that. A large piece with a seat that served as a place to have greenery that could be enjoyed when you sat or simply walked into the room. Joey had been on him about putting plants inside as she'd done on the outside since they'd moved in. He just didn't want to spoil the openness of the lobby. He watched when she pulled out a pad of paper from her bag and pencil. She sat on the floor and began to draw. He simply watched her from a distance and wondered if he should bring up her son. Then thought what the hell, she was aware he knew already.

"Why doesn't your agent know about Benny?" he asked. She stilled in her drawing but then continued. "In fact, no one seems to know about him. It's as if you have separate lives concerning him."

"And it will stay that way, too. Benny is none of your concern. He's mine." She continued drawing as she spoke. "My personal life is nothing to you beyond what you've blackmailed me into."

He nearly lashed out at her about the term "blackmail" but knew that was just what he'd done. He leaned against the wall just a few feet away from her and wondered if bringing up Carver was a good idea. But she spoke first.

"One of the stipulations for me working for you will be that you forget about him. He's very special to me, and I'll

51

not have you blabbing to everyone you know about him."

"Do you know who his father is?" He wouldn't have asked her that if it was her son. He had a feeling she would not have casual sex and would know every man she'd slept with. She didn't answer him.

"This is what I think would work here for you," she said as she stood up. "The colors would be earth tones, pretty much what you have in here already. I have cobalt that I think would complement your other colors, and when you get some plants picked out with it, I'll make sure my colors go well with them, too."

He looked over the drawing, and his breath caught. Christ, she'd only been sitting there for less than fifteen minutes, and this is what she'd come up with. He looked at her over the pad.

"This is amazing. And I love that you've put some of the plants on the piece as well." He held it up where the piece was going to go and could almost see it. "How long will this take? I'm in no hurry other than to see it complete."

"About three months. I have to throw the base piece in several pieces and line them up. Then I'll have to fire them like that. The kiln I'm working on will be perfect for the sheer size of this, but I have to finish it, too." She took back the pad and handed him the sheet after tearing it off. "Give that to your florist of choice and let me know through Rachel what she comes up with. The only color I can see is the blue, the rest will be between her and you."

She was standing so close. He found himself staring at her mouth while she spoke, and he could only moan when she licked her lips. His gaze went to her eyes. He could see something there, and he found he had to taste her.

"No. Don't," she whispered when he cupped the back of her head to bring her to him. But it was too late; he had to have her.

~~~

Reilly had been kissed before. Not a great deal, but she'd had some mouth action. But this man wasn't just kissing her, he was…taking her. She started to reach up and push him away but was wrapping her hand into his dress shirt before she could get her hand to do what her mind wanted. When he pulled her closer to him, his flush with hers, she moaned. The contact was scintillating; sparks seemed to ignite throughout her body from his. He cupped her breast, and she felt it swell under his hand.

"O'Reilly," he moaned her name, and she felt his thigh press against her mound. "Come home with me. I want to fuck you."

Home. She wanted to go home with him, and that's when she remembered her home. Benny was there. The gate. The phone. She wrenched away from him only to have him reach for her again.

"I have to…we can't…you can't do that. I have to go." She grabbed up her things and was to the door when she realized he'd locked it when they came in. She turned to him when she couldn't get the lock to work for her.

He brushed against her without a word. The electricity from him was almost enough to make her want to go back to where they'd been, but once she was on the outside of the building with him, she took several steps back.

"I'm not going to rape you," he snarled at her. "A simple

no would keep me back."

She nodded but wasn't sure what to say. She was humiliated, and he was angry. Not even sure what to say to him, she started to the car. Stopping her with a jerk on her arm was the only thing that kept her from running away.

"What happened back there? I thought we were connecting, and you run like I've done something heinous."

"I did it. Not...I can't get involved with you. With anyone. I want to live my life like I have been. Alone. It's safer for everyone."

He didn't let her go but stared at her. "Does this have anything to do with the call you apparently received before? The one I asked you about? Is it Carver? Is he the one you're hiding from?"

She knew she paled. All the blood drained from her face in that second. She staggered back, and had he not still been holding her, she would have fallen. *He knew* was all she could think of. He knew that Carver was after her, and she wondered how.

"You won't give Benny to him. I swear to you if you even try, I'll kill you myself. He's my—"

"I'm not going to do anything of the kind." He shook her. "Think. I'm not going to give anyone to that bastard. He's not going to get Benny or you. But you need my help. You can't take on a man like him and expect to come out the victor."

Brave words. She jerked from him and went to her car. When he didn't come with her, she turned back before getting in her car, wondering if he was going to get in and let her take him back to his car.

"You don't trust me. I don't think getting in a car with you right now is smart." She started to speak, but he lifted his hand to stop her. "I'll expect you to be at the Foundation offices on Monday. If that's the only way I can keep an eye on you, so be it. Eight o'clock on Monday, and ask for Kasey or Kylie Hunter. They'll expect you."

"You have to see that I'm right. If you know about Carver, then you know what sort of man he is. He'll hurt you like...I can't let him harm anyone, and he'll not get my son."

"You're wrong. And we both know it. If you have any knowledge of what he is capable of, you know that, as well. He won't stop until he gets whatever it is he's told you, and if you don't know that, you're more naive than I thought."

She drove home on auto-pilot. Things were just fine until she...who was this guy, anyway? What rights did he have to barge into her life and treat her as if she hadn't been dealing with this all along without his interference? She parked in the garage and went to the house. She was so tired of this stress and wondered what it would be like to just let someone else help her with it. She shuddered at that thought. That wasn't going to happen in any lifetime she knew of.

Benny was putting together a salad when she walked in. She wasn't hungry really, but she helped him, anyway. Neither of them said anything as she put burgers on the grill and set some potatoes in the microwave to heat. He was staring at her when she looked up from putting their plates together.

"You should know that when you're upset, I can see it

55

on your face. I read about that one time. You should never play poker." She nodded at his observation and had to look down so he couldn't see her tears. "What happened today with the lunch thingy? Did she fire you?"

"It doesn't work that way. She works for me. And no, I didn't fire her." She looked up at him and tried to smile. "Benny, if I'm screwing up with this, you'd tell me, wouldn't you?"

He looked at her with his blank face. He was good at it and would probably play poker very well. He got up from the table and came to her and hugged her. It was all she could do not to break down.

"You took me when you didn't have to. You probably saved me from being on the streets like I wanted and being killed in ten minutes. You have kept me safe and all that." He stepped back before she was ready and smiled up at her. "Let me have the name of the bastard that made you cry, and I'll beat him up for you."

She decided it was when he flexed his small muscles at her that got her. She gave him another quick hug and then brought the burgers in to the table. He was on his second one when she thought about what had happened at Mr. Hunter's office and decided to give him a watered-down version of what had happened.

"I'm going to be doing a piece for that man you liked. That Mr. Hunter contacted my agent and asked for me. It will go a long way for your college fund." He grinned around his burger at her. "You will be pleased to know that he thinks you're okay, too."

"He wants to meet me? Cool. I can't, I know, but it's

nice that he remembers me." He finished off four of the five burgers, then her potato. She was slicing up the cake he'd baked while she'd been gone when he brought up school.

"I have to turn in an art project by the end of the term. Do you think you could help me with something? I don't want to do a pottery piece. That's been enough for me for a while. I was thinking of something like a drawing."

She told him she'd help, and they worked on ideas after they cleaned up the kitchen. She was turning on the dishwasher when she realized he didn't have any male adults to talk to and wondered if she should talk to the school. Then dismissed the idea as silly. She knew he had male teachers, and she paid enough at the private school for someone to be there for him.

After he went to bed, she went out to the kiln again. A few more days and she'd have it done. After she worked on it until she couldn't do anything else, she went into the studio and started weighing up clay balls to throw the Hunter piece. The sooner she got it finished, and in his building, the sooner he would have to leave them alone. She put her fingers over her mouth where he'd kissed her and sighed. She had a feeling he wasn't going to go away anytime soon, no matter how quickly she got the piece finished.

Chapter 6

Daniel was in his office at ten on Monday morning when his mother came in. She looked happy, but he didn't trust that smile for all the money in the world. She was up to something, and he knew it. He picked up the file he'd been going to give her and started on it.

"There are two investments that the corporation should look into. I got word of them over the weekend." When he'd been able to think of something other than O'Reilly and her mouth, that was. "I think it would be something for you to get into."

"I met her this morning." He cocked a brow at her. "The potter. She came by the Foundation when I was there with Kylie. My goodness, she's a pretty little thing, isn't she? And she looked so gorgeous in that little skirt that I immediately thought of Kasey in one like it. I want to go shopping soon."

He put down the file. The thought of O'Reilly in a skirt nearly had him groan. She looked so good in a pair of jeans, he was nearly salivating to see what she'd looked like in a skirt. He looked at his mom and tried to think why she'd come to see him when she'd spoken to —

"Did she…was she nasty to you? If she was, so help me, I'll wring her pretty little neck. She can be mad at me all she wants, but she will not take it out on my family." He knew he'd said too much when she raised both brows at him. "Don't, Mom."

"Don't what? Don't wonder how a woman like her would piss you off. And yes, she's pissed at you. I love you, son, and I just thought…I'll call her and cancel. It's just not worth it. I won't have someone around who might cause you grief on something so dear to our hearts." He shook his head. "It matters to me about this art foundation, but never as much as you do to me."

He closed his eyes, trying to figure out how to explain. He thought if he told her the truth, he'd be in more hot water than if he lied. He knew that lying never got anyone anywhere.

"I kissed her. And before you jump to a conclusion that involves a wedding cake and invitations, she doesn't like me…and not because of…that. She feels as if I'm interfering in her life, and she doesn't…there's a problem, one that I want to help her with. And she won't allow it."

"And that's going to stop you how? You like her?" He nodded. "Well, how much do you…a child. I think I heard someone say she had a child. Is that what this is all about? You are not going to pursue her because of a child?"

"No. Well, I…sort of. I don't care for getting involved with women with children." He sighed. "I *won't* get involved with women with kids. They can get you where you can't simply break it off. And besides, I don't know this kid other than a few minutes with him. And I won't if she has anything to do with it. There's a problem. A huge problem, and she won't let me get close to either of them for fear of someone finding him."

He knew he'd told her too much. He did trust his mom, and he needed someone to talk to. The more he thought about O'Reilly, the more he...he wanted more than a one-nighter with her.

"If it helps you at all, I've spoken to Doyle. And your brothers. They think that she is running from this man who killed her sister. Are you afraid he'll...well, come after you if you're involved with her?"

"No," he nearly shouted. He took a deep calming breath. "No. I'm not worried about that at all. I'm not getting 'involved' with anyone, especially not her. And Doyle had no right to go to you with this. This is between her and me."

"If you believe that everything that affects you doesn't affect the rest of us, then you're not my son. We are a family, and we stick together. If someone messes with someone in this family, even if she is someone you just want to have a bout of sex with, then it affects all of us." She sat up straighter in the chair. "Is that all she is to you? If she is, then I have to agree with her. Keep away. No amount of sex is good enough to get you hurt."

She had a point, but he was afraid it was too late for that. There was something about O'Reilly that.... "She drives me insane. I can't seem to stop thinking about her, and she doesn't want a thing to do with me. Then there is Benny.

He seemed like a good kid. I didn't get to talk to him much, but...do you remember that kid I used to bring over all the time when I was a kid?"

His mom nodded. "Gilbert Shane. Nice boy. Terrified of his shadow most of the time. He was also...." She looked up at him sharply. "You think someone hurt him?"

"I don't know. And I doubt if it's sexual. It's more...like I said, I didn't talk to him much, but she's hiding him for a reason. I've read up on this Carver person, and I believe he's capable of all sorts of heinous things, but sexually abusing a boy? I don't know."

His mom stood. "I'll invite her to the house. She'll be to dinner on Sunday, as will you. I don't care if...I will have the boy there, too. And if there is anything we can do to help him, then we'll do it regardless of what she wants. I can move mountains, and one little girl is not going to give me any problems."

After she left his office, he smiled. He wasn't too sure, but he thought maybe his mom might have a better time moving a mountain than O'Reilly. She was tougher than she might think.

~~~

"No, thanks. I have to get home." It was Friday, and Reilly was exhausted. She hadn't been sleeping well, and she'd burned her back the day before, messing with the kiln again. She tried not to wince every time she moved, but Benny had been having more nightmares, and he was keeping her awake with worry.

"It's just dinner, for heaven's sake. Come to dinner on Sunday, and we'll talk about the progress of all the students you'll start with on Monday." Kylie wasn't whiny. She was simply annoying, and she'd been asking the same thing every day since Monday. "My family wants to meet you."

"I'm pretty sure I've met them all this week. It's been a big parade here since I started. Now if you don't mind, I have to go home. I have things to do if I'm going to be here next week." Reilly knew it was an idle threat. She'd been enjoying herself helping put the finishing touches on the project there. She'd even enjoyed talking to the woman teaching the art end of the school.

"You might as well give it up, Kylie love, she won't come because of me." She turned to see Mr. Hunter there. Daniel was the only one she'd not seen two hundred times in the past five days. And their mother had been by the most.

"I don't give two shits about you, so get over yourself. I have things to do, and spending time with the rich and famous isn't high on my list." Plus, he looked too good standing there leaning against the doorjamb in another suit. She wondered if he had anything but suits, and decided she wasn't going to care.

He moved into the room she and Kylie had been in and closed the door. He moved to her slowly, and she had to really restrain herself from taking steps backward to get away from him. He was just too sure of himself, and she wasn't thrilled about the way he made her feel.

"My family hasn't mentioned it, but they are aware of your son." His voice was low, but she knew that Kylie had heard him. She was nodding. "They don't, however, know what he is to you, really."

This was a whisper, the barest movement of his mouth.

But she heard him. She did take a step back now and bumped into the wall. The cry that spilled from her lips was sharp, and she came forward and into his chest before she could think to sidestep from him. He had her turned and shirt up before she could breathe through the pain and tell him to leave her alone.

"Christ, what did you do? Kylie, go and get the nurse, will you?" To her, he said to stand still. "What did you do, back into a fire? This looks infected."

"I'm fine." She wasn't, and she was pretty sure he knew it, too. "I'm fine and just want to go home. Let me go."

"If I have to bend you over my knee to make sure you know how much I want you to mind right now, so help me, I will. When did you do this?" She told him Monday, and he cursed again. "Were you, I don't know, going to see anyone about this before you died of some horrible infection?"

"I don't know how many times I have to tell you that I'm fine before you start to understand. *I'm fine.*" She had shouted the last two words, but she was pretty sure they'd lost their effect when she sobbed, too.

He walked around to face her, holding her tightly in his hands. "Don't cry, baby. The nurse is going to have a look at it. And if she says you're fine, I'll believe her."

Reilly wanted to point out that she would know more about herself than a nurse would, but only nodded. She was hurting...and badly. She felt cool hands at her back and someone speaking low to her. She couldn't understand the words, but the soothing-ness of them helped the pain.

"O'Reilly, look at me." She hadn't realized that she'd closed her eyes and swayed a little when she opened them.

The pain was nearly overwhelming her now. "Where is Benny? Is he home or somewhere else?"

"He's...why?" She couldn't think. The nurse was saying something about infection and antibiotics. Her body started to tremble, and she could feel something trickle down her back. "What is that?"

"You burst a blister when you hit the wall. She said that you're lucky to be standing. I'm going to have to go and get Benny. You're not going to be able to go home. You're going to the hospital."

"*No*," she screamed in panic. "He's got to be safe. He'll know what to do if I can't come home. But I am. The hospital will...he will be terrified if I take him there. His mother...I have to go to him. Mr. Hunter, please just let me go."

He rested his head against hers, and she felt a small pinch in her arm. "I can't love. I'm going to give you your phone, and you tell him to come with me. The nurse has given you something for the pain, and we'll take care of you. I will go and get him and bring him to my house. I swear to you he'll be as safe as he would be with you."

She felt herself slipping and knew it was only a matter of time before she was out. Did she trust this man? It seemed she had no choice. She took her cell phone and pressed the only number programmed in it. He answered on the first ring.

"It's Mom. I'm sending Mr. Hunter to get you. He'll know the word. You understand?" She could hear his harsh intake of breath before he spoke.

"Are you hurt?" She told him yes, her back. "I'll come with him. I'll be ready." She hung up and looked at the man in front of her.

"If you hurt him or allow him to even break a fingernail, I will hunt you down and kill you slowly. Do you understand me?" She heard his mother behind her but didn't stop now. She was fading fast. "It's sierra. You say sierra to him, and he'll go with you."

"Sierra. I got it." Then he pulled her to him and kissed her hard on the mouth. "And I won't hurt him. You will trust me on this."

The world blacked out. She knew she was falling, not to the floor, but into the blackness quickly. She had a moment of panic, then quiet. And the last thought she had was. *Finally, I'll be able to sleep.*

She felt fuzzy when she opened her eyes. She could see feet moving below her. The movement made her sick. Someone said, "She's coming back again." Someone else cursed. She had to smile. This person had a very good grasp of stringing together bad words. Then she was out again.

Chapter 7

Benny waited near the house. He knew that she'd called him to tell him Mr. Hunter was coming, but he still had no desire to be caught in the house again if someone came in. The last time with his real mom had been bad enough. The gate was open for him, and all he needed now was the password to leave. He hoped she was all right.

He knew she'd been hurt. The first night it had happened, he heard her cry out. But when he'd gone to her to see if he could help, she'd told him she was fine. He knew that she wasn't, but she kept telling him to go inside, and she'd be in soon. Then this morning, he'd had a hard time waking her up. He thought she'd been dead until she looked up at him with her eyes all glassy looking.

His real mom had done drugs. He wasn't stupid to think that she hadn't. He knew what a person looked like when they were full of something bad. His aunt didn't look like that. She looked like she hurt. And when she moved, she

66

looked like it hurt her really bad. He tensed up when he heard a car pull into the circle driveway.

He recognized Mr. Hunter, but he didn't know the woman with him. She was old, and Benny wondered if it was his girlfriend. Then Mr. Hunter called her "Mom" and told her to wait there while he went to the house. Before he could get to the porch, Benny stepped out from behind the garage.

"You startled me." He smiled at him, but Benny wasn't ready to trust just yet. "Your mom sent me to get you. They took her to the hospital, and she's going to be all right. But she didn't want you to be left here to worry."

"I wouldn't. She will come home to me." At least he hoped she would. He loved her, but he still remembered what it was like when his real mom would leave him for days, sometimes weeks at a time to go to that man.

Mr. Hunter nodded. "Well, come on. I'm taking you to my house. And my mom is going to go with us. I don't know a great deal about kids, and I know your mom keeps you safe."

"No." Benny wasn't sure how this was supposed to work, as he'd never had to use the code word before, but he knew that he couldn't ask him for it. That was something she'd drilled in his head for hours one day. "I'll be all right here."

The man took a step toward him, and Benny clutched his pack back tighter to him. If the man wanted to, Benny knew he could bring him down. He just hoped it wouldn't come to that.

"I'm sorry. I forgot. Sierra. I'm supposed to tell you

sierra." He put out his hands, palms up and wide apart. "Will you come with me now?"

Benny felt the tension and terror roll off him. He was nearly dizzy with relief. Before he could take a step toward him, the woman came from behind Mr. Hunter. He looked at her, then back at Mr. Hunter.

"This is my mom. Annemarie Hunter. Mom, this is Benton Harlequin, O'Reilly's son." He moved slowly toward him and reached for the bag at his feet, not touching the one Benny had in his arms. "Come on, Benny. I'll take you to my house. Then we'll see if we can get some information on your mom."

He got into the little car. The back of it was barely big enough for him to fit in with his backpack, but he sat sideways and buckled. The man and the woman sat in the front, and both of them buckled, too. Mr. Hunter turned around to back up and winked at him.

"I don't know how to cook kid stuff, so we'll either order out or see what I can throw together from the freezer, okay?" Benny nodded.

"I can cook. Mom said all men should cook in case the woman they meet can't. She can cook pretty good, but I make better spaghetti sauce." He didn't know why he said that and looked away before continuing. "And she don't like to be called O'Reilly. It's just Reilly."

"She *doesn't* like to be called O'Reilly. And I know. That's why I do it." He stopped at the end of the drive and looked at Benny. "Will the gate lock up, or do I have to do something to engage it?"

"I set it on fry when we leave." He flushed. "The power

is on. And she does that, too. Corrects me. Can't a man have any peace from learning something?"

The older woman laughed, and Benny thought it the nicest sound he'd ever heard. His aunt laughed with him all the time, but this woman laughed without him making a joke. Not that Reilly did, but the kids at school sometimes did when he got better grades than them. He looked out the window and asked about his aunt.

"Mr. Hunter, is she going to die?" He didn't look at the man until he was quiet for so long. He was looking at him in the mirror in front of him. "Is she?"

"No. She has a bad infection from the burn on her back. Did you know she'd done that?" Benny nodded and waited for him to yell at him, but he didn't. "I thought so. It must have been hard for her to hide it from you so you'd not worry. But in answer to your question, she's not going to die. She's sick, but with the proper care, which I will promise she'll get even if she doesn't think she needs it, she'll be up to her old grumpy self in no time. And, Benny, I'd very much like it if you called me Daniel. Mr. Hunter is my brother. He's the old one."

Benny didn't understand the man's laughter when his mom hit him. It wasn't hard, Benny supposed, but still, when his mom had hit him, she'd been a lot meaner. He leaned back in his seat and thought about where he was going.

He didn't know this man or his family, but he didn't make him feel nervous. There was something very…calming about the man. The woman, too, if Benny thought about it. Mr. Hunter, or Daniel, seemed like a nice guy, but Benny was aware that people wore all kinds of costumes and what sort they pulled out was how he reacted to them. Benny was waiting to see how this man was dressed before he let his guard down too much.

The house they pulled in front of was huge. When he'd lived in Florida with his mom, they'd lived in this big building, too, but this was very different. This one had one person living in it, while the other place had about a million. And he'd bet his last allowance money that there wasn't a rat within a hundred miles of this place.

This one had a nice garden in the front. Flowers were everywhere, and Benny figured that he'd make a mint off this guy just watering them all. The front of the house was big, too, with four big columns holding up the top of a porch-like thing. The windows gleamed in the sun, and he wondered how many people lived here with him. When they pulled into the garage, Benny knew it had to be at least six if the number of cars and motorcycles had any bearing on it. He said as much to the man.

"No. I like cars and collect them. The bike I've had since high school and couldn't part with it when I started making money. It depends on where I'm going and what I plan to do when I get there on what I take. But the bike is for special occasions."

"My mom has just the one car. She said she could get a new one, but that's just a waste of money if you can only drive one at a time." He flushed when the woman laughed. "I'm sorry. I didn't mean that you waste your money, sir."

He ruffed up his hair and told him not to worry. "I'm the butt of someone's joke all the time. My brothers all sold their fun cars when they got married. So since I never plan

70

to marry, I can keep my toys for as long as I want."

Benny was shown to a room and then was told where Daniel slept. "If you need anything, I'm right there." Then he told him that it was just the two of them in the house if you didn't count his friend and cook, Roger.

Roger was a huge man, Benny found out later, and he thought the man was sweet on Mrs. Hunter. He got bright red every time he spoke to her and stammered all over his words whenever he spoke to her. Benny thought it was stupid to like girls. They smelled pretty sometimes, but so not worth the effort. He decided that Daniel had the right idea: don't ever get married, and you would never have to sell your stuff.

He had a dinner of grilled cheese and a bowl of tomato soup. Roger said that no self-respecting person ate soup from a can when Benny had asked what brand it was. He had no idea what that had meant and didn't ask again. He figured the guy was nuts or very possessive of his food names. Benny told him it was the best he'd ever eaten. And it was.

"Roger is a cordon bleu chef. He works for me until something better comes along." Daniel sat next to Benny and leaned toward him as he finished speaking. "He's been telling me that for years, and yet he's still here."

This was a weird house, Benny concluded later when Daniel and Roger argued over the best kind of cheese to make a sandwich with and how to slice the bread when making one. Benny and Reilly simply pulled the bread out of the bag and used it. They didn't care much how it was sliced so long as it was. He told them that when asked his opinion.

"Heathens," Roger said. "I will fatten your girlfriend up when she comes to stay with us in a few days. That will stop this baggage bread nastiness."

"Mom is your girlfriend?" Soup halfway to his mouth sloshed on the table. "I don't think…she doesn't need a boyfriend. I take care of her fine when she lets me. And you can't be her boyfriend," he suddenly realized. "You don't come over and knock her around when she makes you mad."

Benny knew he'd made a big mistake the moment he'd realized what he'd said. He looked around at the silent people and started to stand. He'd leave before he let this guy hit him, too.

"Sit, Benny. No one here is going to knock anyone around. And your…mom isn't my girlfriend. She can barely stand me enough to let me near her, much less…besides, I think your mom can kick my a…butt if I made her mad enough."

Benny sat, but he was no longer hungry. He looked at the phone on the wall and wondered if he could call her. Mrs. Hunter came into the room then and sat across from him.

"I just spoke with your mom's doctor, and they said she is doing fine but will be out of it until tomorrow afternoon. He is concerned about how bad the burn is, but says that other than a few small scars she'll be fine. Do you know how she did it?"

"She was building that kiln and had to burn off some of the wiring that she didn't need. She said that she'd gotten it hotter than she meant to, and when she tripped over some of the kiln bricks, she'd fallen against the hot wall of other bricks. She gets burned all the time, but it's always little stuff." Benny hugged his pack to his side. "She said if she ever gets hurt enough to be in the hospital that I didn't have to come see her. She knows I hate hospitals."

But he found he wanted to see her, to make sure she was all right and she wasn't hurt like his mom had been. He looked at the phone again, and then Daniel spoke up.

"I'll go and see her tomorrow and send you a picture of her from her bed. If she's awake, you can speak to her, and she'll tell you she'll be fine herself." Benny nodded and yawned. "Why don't we get you up to your room and to bed? It's been a long day, and I'm sort of tuckered out myself."

Mrs. Hunter left before he went upstairs while Roger went to his rooms. Daniel stood at the bottom of the stairs and watched the cook go up. Benny turned to look at Daniel one more time and came to a hasty decision.

"You know, don't you? That she's not my mom." It wasn't a question, but Daniel nodded anyway. "Then why are you taking me in like this? Do you want to get into her pants like that man who hurt her did by trying to be nice to me?"

Daniel didn't come up the stairs and hit him like he expected him to, but he did lean against the handrail. "That's very crude, and you know it. What would O'Reilly think if she heard you speak like that? Or better yet, what should I think if you'll speak to me so disrespectfully?"

Benny wanted to cry. He'd meant to make the man mad at him, but now he wasn't sure why. He dropped his head and snapped it back up when Daniel told him to look at him when he was being spoken to.

"I don't want to be here." That wasn't quite right, so he tried again. "I saw what he did to her. My real mom. I saw how he…he beat her with a bat before he let those men have her like an animal. Then they all got to punch on her while she was screaming."

Daniel was up the stairs in a second and pulled Benny into his arms. "I'm so sorry, Benny. I didn't know you'd been witness to that. What did your aunt say when you told her?"

"I didn't. I've not told her anything." He looked up at the man and scrubbed at his tears. "You won't, either. I can't let that man have what he wants. If I do, there ain't nothing left for me to keep him away. If he knows what I have, he'll let me go if I give it back to him, right?"

Daniel didn't answer, and Benny was sure it was because he was trying to figure out how to get rid of him before that man came here. He pulled away and felt as if someone had taken a warm blanket from his heart.

"I'll go back to the house now, please. There are plenty enough boxes of stuff there for me to eat until she comes back."

"You're not going anywhere. Christ. You and your aunt are the most…why do you think I want you to go? Because I don't. But as I've told your aunt, I can't help you if you don't tell me what's going on. Who is this bastard, and why is he threatening O'Reilly?"

"He's calling her? You think…. Oh gosh, he was the one who was at the gate that day. She said it was a glitch, but

74

I told her someone stole the remote thingy. Now he can... she changed it. That's why she puts it on fry all the time. To keep him out."

Benny was suddenly terrified for his aunt. He started down the stairs, thinking he could probably walk to the hospital; it couldn't really be that far. When the man was blocking the door, Benny thought maybe he'd hit him and leave, but he was handing him his coat.

"Come on. We'll go and keep an eye on her together. I have a few friends and family to call in to keep her safe when I can't be at two places at once. You okay with going to the hospital with me?"

Daniel made a lot of calls on the way over to the hospital. And this time they rode in a big SUV.

Chapter 8

Humberto Carver twirled his knife on its tip round and round as he thought about what the man in front of him had said. He couldn't get past the gates again. Berto, as he was called by those brave enough to consider him their friend, looked at the pictures that had accompanied the man. The dead man, it now seemed.

"I took him over there and had him try out the fence like you told me to. He was right. It was fired up, all right." The other man, Micky Lynch, laughed at his own joke. "I don't think anybody is going to figure out what it was that hit the fence, much less who it was."

"So, there isn't an opening?"

Micky said, "No."

"How am I supposed to get what this sister has of mine if she doesn't come out of her cave, and there is a hotwire around the place all the time?" He didn't expect an answer and wasn't surprised when none was forthcoming.

"There aren't even any cleaning services or nothing coming in either. I tried to find out if they had a cook or something, but there ain't nobody. I'm thinking they's a lot more domestic than her big sister ever was."

That was true. Meagen couldn't boil water without making a mess and using every pot in the kitchen. And she was worse at cleaning up said mess. No, they were nothing alike when it came to that. He laid his knife down, steepled his fingers in front of his face, and tried to remember if Meagen had ever mentioned she had a sister.

Meagen had been his main woman in his harem of fifty-plus bitches. She'd keep them in line and high enough that they never cared about how badly he hurt them when he fucked them. Berto liked it rough, and not only that, he liked to fuck women until they were dead. It was a turn-on for him.

Then she'd disappeared. He'd thought about letting her go with just her death, but...well, he didn't like it when someone decided *they* were through. That was his decision. He'd found her coming out of a clinic less than a year later. A clinic that was known for its abortion practices.

She'd admitted that she'd waited nearly too long to have the abortion and now was paying the price. She'd been bleeding badly when he brought her back, and it had taken her nearly two months to get over it. Then when she had, he'd nearly killed her for leaving him. After that, she'd been helpful to him, but no longer held the same sexual appeal she had before. He let her have her own place to keep her sad-looking face from being around him. Then the books and money had come up missing.

77

He knew it had been her. He'd had a camera on the vault since he'd had it set up. How she'd gotten in and out without setting off alarms had taken him nearly a month to figure out. Then when he had, she'd been stupid enough to die before she'd been able to tell him where his stuff was. And now he realized how much more she'd taken than just a few cooked-up books and some money, but she'd taken his list.

"I want all you can find on the sister. I could care less about the old man. Who does she date? Where she buys her tampons? I want it all. And there'd better not be a single surprise, either, when I catch up with our little potter's wife." He picked up the knife again and put it into the drawer and pulled out a thick envelope. "There's enough in there to bribe the tightest lipped person you find. Get it for me."

"All right, boss. You want I should snatch her if I get the chance? Might be easier to ask her some things if she ain't behind that gate of hers."

"No. I want to be able to walk up to her and put a bullet in her head if I find she's been spending my money like it was hers." He waited until Micky was out of the room before he continued. "And if they've made a deal with the Feds, there won't be a place she can hide that I won't find her and make her pay."

Berto pulled out the little file at the bottom of his desk. Some of the pictures in there made him smile. He'd been glad when he'd thought of taking pictures of Meagen when they'd finished with her. Dropping her off at the emergency room had been a mistake, he knew that now. But who would have thought that she'd live as long as she had? The doctor

78

knew nothing and the cop who'd been called in less than that. He glanced at the picture of the two men when he'd gotten all he could out of them. And neither of them had mentioned a sister. Even though she'd been there to talk to his Meagen.

Of course, his anger had been out of control. He'd killed the cop before he'd had the thought to ask if anyone had come to see her. He'd gone on and on about how she'd been out of her head when he'd talked to her. The doctor had lasted a bit longer. And he'd mentioned someone had come to speak to her, but she'd not been there long enough to say much; the woman, Meagen he'd called her, had died only a minute or two after the younger woman had come to the bed. That he calling her Meagen was what had pissed Berto off enough to kill him faster than he'd meant to. But he still managed to have some fun with him. Murder his way was such a blast.

And now that he'd figured out who this O'Reilly Harlequin was and that he had the one person who might have the information he needed, he couldn't get to either of them. He looked up when someone knocked on his door and was surprised to see his newest acquisition.

Jeannie Whitney was as beautiful as she was smart. And her ingeniousness in bed sometimes outdid even him. He'd never tell her, of course, but he smiled when she came to him and knelt before him. Christ, if she took him in her mouth now, he'd come immediately. He had a feeling she knew it, too. But before he'd let her see him as a weaker man, he pushed her away from him and growled low.

"When I want a blow job, I'll call you. Right now, I'm not

in the mood." She glanced at his hard cock but said nothing. "I want you to get someone to go to Ohio. There has to be someone there you can recruit for me."

"Sex or favors? And do you want a female this time, or will a male do?" He looked away, trying to concentrate on her words and not the way her dress rode up her thighs and her bare legs were open to him.

"Female and favors with the possibility of sex. I need her to see if she can seduce an old man into coming out of hiding. There's a woman I want in that compound, and she is what I want."

Jeannie nodded and opened her legs wider. "When?" she asked as she moved her hand down her body. "Do I go now or…later?"

He wanted her to go now before he gave into her. And she knew it.

"Come here," he growled. She moved up to her knees and then moved like a slick cat up his body to his groin. He could see that she was aroused; her juices had been teasing him for five minutes. "Suck me off and make it good."

Without a word, she unzipped his pants. When she reached into his trousers and pulled him free, she licked him from root to tip. She was going to make him come, and he wasn't going to be happy if he did it on her face and not her throat. He scooted down in the chair and watched as she took him into her mouth.

"Christ." He grabbed a handful of her hair and pulled her down over him hard. She swallowed him, and the tightening around his cock nearly sent him over the edge. His balls tightened up, and he could feel his climax start to tingle there. Before he could tell her to slow down, she grabbed his balls and twisted.

He was shooting his load down her gullet before he could think. More, he needed more. Jerking her up by her hair, he slammed her head on his desk as he jerked her skirt up over her hips. When she opened her legs for him, he opened her ass up and buried himself in her tight hole. Her scream made him see stars, and before he knew it, he was coming again. Christ, he'd never had this much fun with a woman before.

Spent, he sat down in his chair after adjusting his clothes. Jeannie got up off his desk and left the room. She would do as he told her to and not complain a minute about it, much like she did when he fucked her without giving her release. He was also pretty sure she would get it elsewhere and didn't ask. He normally didn't share, but he feared she'd kill him if he had to have sex with her as often as she liked. The woman was insatiable.

~~~

Reilly woke slowly. She felt as if she was coming up from a great fog, and it wasn't dissipating as quickly as she thought it should. The voices sounded familiar, but nothing she could place. Opening one eye, she quickly closed it again, thinking she was dreaming.

"Wake up and have something to eat. The doctor said as soon as you eat a good meal, I can take you home with me." She peered at Mr. Hunter and groaned his name. "And stop calling me that. I've had you wrapped around me and your tongue down my throat. I think that qualifies us for first name basis."

"Where is Benny? You said…." She had to swallow twice and was startled when a spoonful of ice was shoved in her mouth. "Stop that. What are you doing here?"

"I'm right here. Daniel and I have been watching over you." Daniel? What was Mr. Hunter doing there still? She tried to sit up, but the pain in her back stilled her. "The doctor said you'd hurt for a bit, but you'd be okay soon."

She tried her best to bring him into focus, but all she could see were hazy shapes. She had to close her eyes or be sick. It wasn't until Mr. Hunter spoke again that she opened them all the way.

"Open up. Come on, take in some more ice. The nurse said it would feel good on your throat." She opened her mouth to yell at him to go away. But all she got for her effort was a mouth full of cold water. "I have to speak to you, and I don't have a lot of time before Benny comes back."

"You said you'd watch over him." She had to swallow again as he shoved another spoon of liquid into her. "You do that again, and I'm going to shove that spoon so far up your ass you're never going to find it."

He leaned down and took her lower lip into his mouth and nipped. She looked at him wide-eyed when he stood up. Then, just as quickly, he leaned back to her and took her entire mouth.

The man could kiss. She felt the burn of his mouth all the way to her toes. When his tongue brushed over her lips, she opened for him and moaned when he danced his tongue along hers.

"You make it difficult to think when you moan like that. Well, thinking isn't so hard, it's the thoughts that

I'm thinking that make me hard." He stood slowly again, and she watched as he adjusted his hard cock. "I've been thinking about doing that for hours. Just wanting to take a nibble out of you."

"You wanted to tell me something," she reminded him. Thinking about his body and his mouth was making her dizzy. She tried to blame it on the pain, but to be honest, she never felt it while he was kissing her.

"Your son...Christ, I want you." He took a step back, and then another before he sat in the chair. "Benny knows now that you've been threatened. And before you get your panties in a twist, he figured it out. I didn't tell him. He seems to think someone stole your remote to the gates. Did they?"

"I simply misplaced it." He glared, and she turned her face from his. "I know how to take care of us. You and your family are the most annoying people I've met. Did you know that they have it in their heads that you're...let me see what did she call it? Oh yeah, 'sweet on me.' Who says that?"

"That would be my sister-in-law Kylie. She is sort of old fashioned, and her dad...this has nothing to do with anything. And they think if I get married or whatever they can rub my face in it and tell me they told me so." He took a deep breath. "Back to your issue. Humberto Carver, have you ever heard of him?" Yes, her mind screamed, but she said nothing to him. He continued. "He's been linked to your sister in a few things that the Feds are looking into. And a couple of them think...they wonder if you and him hooked up, and that's where Benny came from."

She looked at him, then away. It took her several months

to figure it out, and he had it in less than a week. Maybe if she refused to answer him, he'd get mad and leave. Reilly glanced at him, then back at the television set. No, he'd not leave. He was worse than a dog with a bone.

The door opened, and Benny came in, his arms loaded with bags. She watched as Mrs. Hunter came in with the other three Hunter women. She held Benny's hand as she glared at the people in her room.

"I appreciate you watching my son for me, but I'm going to go home now, and I'll be taking him with me. Thank you so much for your—"

"Bullshit." They all looked over at the older woman. "Yes, I said it, and you all know it. This is no longer a matter for you to try and take on yourself, young lady. The Hunters take care of their own. Now hush up and tell us—"

"You leave my aunt alone." The room tensed when Benny spoke. "She's been taking care of me better'n anyone ever did before. I have to do my homework now, and I have a house, not a crappy hole to live in. If she tells you she's got this, then you'd better bet she does. She's the best in the whole wide world."

Before she could tell Benny to apologize to them all, Daniel clapped his hands. Then Curtis and the women joined them. Benny moved to her bed and held her hand tighter. She started to get up and was pressed back to the bed by Daniel. He moved his face to her ear and whispered low to her.

"Get up again, and I'll think you're well enough to help me with my problem from earlier." He bit her earlobe, and she moaned. "Behave."

"I, for one, want to tell you what a good boy you are, young man. It's commendable of you to want to protect your aunt that way and to stand up for what you believe in." Then Mrs. Hunter pointed her finger at him. "You should also know that I don't care for impertinent children. But in your case, I'll accept that you're under a good deal of stress. Doyle, tell us what you know."

Reilly looked over at the large man she'd not seen until that moment. He grinned at her, then winked. He handed her a thick file, then one to the rest of the people in the room. Daniel curled up on her bed behind her and held open the file with her. She wanted to tell him to back off, but the first thing in the folder made her heart stop.

"I asked the young Harlequin here if he wanted to not see the pictures. He said he'd...he told me that he saw his momma getting beat up that day, and he thought these pictures couldn't hurt as bad as the real thing. He looked at them, and after he had a few minutes to himself, he decided to help me."

"Help you?" Reilly looked over at her nephew. "Help him how? You never wanted to talk about this before. Why now?"

Reilly tried not to let the hurt show, but she knew she wasn't doing so hot at it. He sat on the chair next to her bed and took her hand again. He showed her the first picture, the one from the hospital when she'd seen her sister in all that blood.

"Because he might do this to you. And I can't stand to lose you. You're...you're all I got, Reilly. And...and I don't want to...." He looked at Daniel, and she wasn't sure what had passed between them, but Benny nodded. "I love you, Reilly. I know I never told you that before, but I do. I think I loved you before that night you took me away. I can't let that man do what he did to my mother to you."

"He won't. Not if I have anything to say about it." Doyle told them to open the file to the last half. "This is all we have on Humberto Carver. He goes by the name of Berto to most of those who know him. He has a house in Florida where up until about ten years ago, your sister lived with him. She moved out around the time you were supposedly giving birth to this young man. From Paris. And he was born in North Dakota."

Reilly flushed. "I, as you know, didn't have Benny. I didn't even know he existed until I was called to her bedside, and she told me that I had to go pick up something she'd left me. She told me it was where I'd found her once before. I didn't know what to expect. I thought it was going to be... honestly, I didn't have a clue, but a boy wasn't it."

"How did you know where to go?" She looked at Curtis when he asked. "The doctor wrote in his report that she was out of her head on something and that she was in a great deal of pain. He didn't even mention you in his report to the police. And the cop, a...let me see," he referred to his file. "Nickolas, Officer Nickolas, wrote in his that no one had been with her when she'd died."

"I made it, but I'd only just made it. She told me that I had to go where we'd met when I was sixteen. And when I started to mention the name, she'd cut me off, as if she didn't trust who heard. I can see now that she was probably right." Reilly looked at Benny as she continued. "She told me to keep it safe. Made me promise."

"We'd been practicing. She'd tell me to go and get myself a piece of pie or something when he came over to her. She never let him see me, but I saw him a few times. When the men came to the house the last time and asked her about some money, she'd not had time to get me out the window. I hid in the closet near the door. I could hear them, all of them asking her where it was and why'd she taken it. Then the man came in and…. After they left, I waited and climbed out the window to the fire escape. I stayed there until I saw them leave with her in a bunch of our towels. When they was gone, I jumped down and went to the diner like she told me to do if anything happened to her."

"Christ. You were in the room with her when they did this to her?" Royce asked. Benny nodded. "You're a hell of a kid. I don't think I could have…what happened to the money? Do you know if it was ever recovered?"

Benny shook his head and said nothing. Reilly knew he was lying, and she was pretty sure that at least Daniel knew it, too. She didn't say anything then and decided the first opportunity she got she was going to ask him about the backpack.

Chapter 9

Daniel was at the hospital the next morning when she was being checked out by the doctor. She didn't say anything to him, but he didn't care. He was going to win this battle with her because possession was nine-tenths of the law. He grinned when she asked if a cab could be called. Daniel nodded to the doctor as he left the room.

"I have your ride. And the nice policeman that has been keeping an eye on you for me will help me carry your things out to my car. Benny is at school, so we have plenty of time to get you settled." He took the pillow from her when she looked like she was going to hit him with it. "Once we get you home, we can play then if you're up to it. But for now, I need you to get dressed."

"I'm not going to your home. I have a perfectly good home that I own. I thank you for your time, but fuck off." She'd said it so sweetly that he found himself laughing.

"No, my dear, I want to fuck you. Hard, fast, slow, on

the table, on the floor, anywhere and everywhere we can."

Her mouth snapped shut. He wasn't sure what she was thinking, but he was reasonably sure that it involved body parts, mostly his and lots of blood. He helped her to the bathroom with as much touching of her as he could and stood outside the door when she insisted that he go away.

"A man could get a real complex hanging around you." He was putting her things in the overnight bag he'd brought for her when the door opened. He wasn't sure how it had happened, but he was on the floor, and his head hurt while it seemed as if O'Reilly was flying through the air. He laid his head on the cool floor and closed his eyes. There was something very wrong here.

"I said, are you all right?" He must have dozed off. Yes, that was it. What other reason would O'Reilly have for smacking him around? "Wake up, you moron, I don't know if there is anyone else coming to kill us."

That woke him up. He was standing up again when he realized he was hurting. "Christ, I'm bleeding." The blood on his shirt was starting to make him dizzy again, and he felt his chin being jerked up.

"Look at me. Now I'm going to take us into the hallway, but I want you to…please don't faint on me again."

"I did not faint. I merely settled on the floor to keep it from hitting it overly hard when I needed to fall." That didn't even make sense to him, and he'd said it. "I don't know what happened. Did you fly?"

"Yes. I flew. And the Easter Bunny is coming to visit you." He didn't think there was a reason for her to be snarky, but he did stand up. "I have to make sure she's dead. Can you hold onto the door for me?"

Dead? He looked down at the woman, a nurse actually, and saw that her head was on her shoulders oddly. He stared just long enough to get it.

"Her neck is broken." He was feeling slightly sick now, and when his phone rang, he couldn't seem to make his fingers work. "Here. Tell them I'm sick."

The floor was shifting again when he heard her speak. There was something wrong with his hearing now. Tunnel, it sounded like they were going down a long tunnel. He pulled O'Reilly to him by cupping the back of her head and leaning his head against hers.

"Your brother is coming. I'm so sorry. You shouldn't have been here, and you wouldn't have gotten shot." He was surprised by that. He'd been shot? "I'm going to let your brother come for you, and you'll be fine. They don't want you, but Benny and me. You'll be all right until he gets here."

He couldn't let her go. He knew if he did, he'd never see her again, and he wasn't sure why that hurt him so much, but he couldn't let go. He told her he was sorry, too, and pitched forward. He knew he should have thought it through better, but it was all he could do in a pinch. When he landed on her, the last thing he heard was her screaming.

Daniel opened his eyes and looked around. His brothers were there and no O'Reilly. He tried to get up, but there was something holding him down. He looked down at the restraints on his wrists.

"Let me go. What the hell are these things doing on me anyway?" He jerked on them again when Royce was suddenly there. "Where's O'Reilly? Something happened to her, and she was leaving."

"You were shot, and she probably saved your ass. What happened? Do you remember?" He rubbed his hand over his belly and felt the padding there. "It wasn't as bad as it could have been. The bullet just grazed your right side and went through and through."

He remembered now. "A nurse came into the room and asked me where Mrs. Harlequin was. I said bathroom. Then she pulled out this gun, and it sort of…O'Reilly came from nowhere and grabbed the nurse and…Christ, she killed her."

"That's pretty much what Reilly said. She said she tried to get you out of the room to somewhere safe, but you were losing blood and talking off your rocker, her words not mine." He looked from Royce to Jesse when he picked up the story.

"I called, and Reilly answered. She said that there was a dead woman in her room and that you were shot. She told me that she was going to move you. Then before I could get her to tell me more, I heard you talking. Man, you were really out of it. Then the screams." Jesse scrubbed his hand over his face as he continued. "That was the most terrifying moment of my life when I couldn't get an answer, and all those screams coming through the line."

"I was in the hospital," Curtis started. "And heard the code called. I knew the room number, so I took off running and calling you at the same time. When I came around the corner from the elevator, the nurses were trying to get into the room. I shoved the door open and saw what appeared to be a nurse with a broken neck and had them call for the police. I could see you two. Reilly was trying to reach the phone, and you were out."

"Where is O'Reilly then? And Benny? Please tell me he's okay. I know I hurt her back when I fell on her, but she was going to leave me, and I...." Daniel looked at his brothers. "Christ, you've no idea what it felt like knowing I'd never see her again."

They grinned before Royce answered. "She's down the hall. There are a couple of police officers outside her room and one in. She's sort of under arrest until we can figure out who the woman she killed was. She wasn't employed here. Benny is at my house with the women. He was pretty scared when he heard someone had come here for her. Kylie is afraid he plans to split without telling his aunt. He had his backpack with him."

"He always has that thing. And don't touch it. I think it might have stuff from his mom. He hangs onto it like it's his lifeline to her." Daniel tossed off the covers and sat up with the help of his brothers. He was pulling on his robe someone had brought in when his mother walked in.

"Good. Go and talk some sense into that woman. She just threw me out of her room and told me that I needed to be down here, not sitting around annoying her." His mom kissed him on the cheek. "I like her. She's going to be a lot of fun."

He was being pushed down toward her room when he thought about O'Reilly and looked over his shoulder at his mom. He didn't want her to get any permanent ideas about O'Reilly.

"She is nothing more than a woman I'd like to have sex with, Mom. And you know that I don't do kids." He heard her sigh as he continued. "I know you don't like what I said, but I have no intention of ever marrying. I just want to have some fun and live vicariously through my brothers and their wives."

The wheelchair stopped, and he turned to look at his mom. Her face was flushed, and he knew she was upset. He didn't know what to say to her and turned around in the chair when she started moving it again. He was coming around the end where his room was again when he realized she'd brought him back.

"Mom, I thought—"

"I'm sure you did. But that woman doesn't need you sniffing at her skirts like some overgrown teenager. Leave her alone if you just want to…want to toy with her. And that young man? He was beginning to look up to you. A blind man could see it. How do you think he's going to feel if you simply leave because you've had enough sex with his aunt?"

"I'm not going to hurt the kid. He's been around the block a few times. I'm sure he knows all about the birds and the bees." He winced when she hit him in the head. "Hitting me doesn't negate the fact that the kid's mom wasn't a nice person. And I'm pretty sure his aunt has dated a few times since he's been living there."

He shifted in the wheelchair at that thought. He had no idea why that bothered him, but he refused to think about what it meant. She was a woman, he was a man. End of story. He realized she'd been talking and turned to his mom.

"…right here until you figure it out. I told her I'd come by and say goodnight. She didn't seem all that thrilled about it, but I keep my promises. They're supposed to either charge her or let her go in the morning."

"Charge her? With what?" Then it occurred to him that she had killed that woman. "She should have a lawyer. I should go and see if I can do anything about—"

"I think she has one. Her agent, Reilly said, was very resourceful. I hope so. It would be a shame if, after saving your life, she had to go to jail." His mom huffed away, leaving him sitting in the middle of the hall as she went down the hall. He realized then that he had no idea what her room number was.

~~~

Reilly watched the door open and almost wished it was someone there to finish her off. The stupid man falling on her hurt her worse than when she'd burned herself in the first place. She rolled to her side to see who it was and groaned. She'd just gotten rid of one Hunter.

"I'm not in the mood for visitors tonight. So whatever you want, I don't. Now go away." When Royce sat in the chair, she closed her eyes. Ignoring him seemed to be the best way to deal with him.

"You saved my brother today. I owe you." She peeked at him and wondered if he'd simply pay her off by going away and leaving her alone. Then he answered her unspoken question. "I'm not going to let you out of my sight until we catch the bastard who tried to kill you two."

"It was probably some person your brother lost a case to, and he's seeking revenge any way he can." She didn't think so, but it was as good as reason as any other.

"Nah. Daniel has never lost a case. He's pretty savvy about the law." He grinned at her. "Good try, though. I would have gone for something like it was a jilted lover or a woman he messed with that had a husband in the background."

She snorted. "Your brother doesn't strike me as the type to dally with married women, nor does he look like the type of man whose lovers wouldn't be his best friend after it was over."

She was startled by his bark of laughter. He leaned back in his chair and pulled out a dark cigar. He didn't light it but simply stared at it and inhaled it deeply before putting it away again.

"Daniel says the same thing. He doesn't like kids either, or so he says. He gets along with my son. In fact, Lee seems to look forward to him coming over. Lee is our son. You should see him, spitting image of his mom. Anyway," he pulled an envelope out of his jacket pocket and took out some paper. "This is from an investigator. He says that Berto Carver is looking for something. He said that your sister took it one night and he's going to find it. The Feds have someone on the inside, and they're waiting to see what it could be that's missing."

"It's Benny. I'm sure of it. That's why as soon as I'm out of here we're going to run. I know that sounds melodramatic, but that's all it is when you get right to it. I'm afraid, and I'm going to run away." He was shaking his head. "You can disagree all you want, Mr. Hunter, but you really can't stop me."

"Sure, I can. Money talks. And while I know you have plenty, you don't have the resources that I do. Nor the manpower." He put the papers on her lap. "That's a subpoena. You can either play by my rules, or I tell them you refused it."

She picked up the blue-covered document. She read enough to know that it was from the FBI and that they were demanding that she turn over everything she had on her sister and the man named Humberto Carver. She tossed it back at him.

"I don't have anything. Unless, of course, you mean her son." Reilly crossed her arms over her chest carefully, mindful of the pain in her back. "You can try to take him, but I want you to know that I will kill you before you get within five feet of him."

"She will too. She has the training." Reilly looked over at her trainer. She grimaced when he sat down next to Royce Hunter. "Hello, darling. How're the workouts going?"

"Doyle, you know her?" Reilly looked from one man to the other, then laid her head back as Royce spoke again. "You have been leading us a merry chase all along."

"No. When I met her, she was calling herself Dawn O'Reilly. I didn't put the two together until this morning when I was in her room. I hadn't thought of you in years," he said to her. "So, I was a little slow on the uptake until I heard Daniel call her by her given name."

"I didn't want to be a victim, so I had someone train me. He was supposed to be quiet about the whole thing. You didn't tell me you worked for the Feds either, so we're pretty much even, I think." She sat up straight in the bed and was about to toss the covers off her when the door opened again. This Hunter wasn't very happy with her either, but she'd had enough of all of them. "It's time you all leave. Now. I'm going to have a lot to do tomorrow, and it doesn't involve happy hour with the Hunter clan."

"Stay there." She heard the anger in Daniel's voice and nearly snapped at him to fuck off when he lifted his finger at her to be quiet. He turned to his brother and Doyle. "I have to stay until tomorrow, and I'm going to spend the night with O'Reilly here. She won't be going anywhere until I say so."

Well, fuck this shit. She got out of the bed and lifted her hands to Doyle when he stepped to her. "Come on, old man. Even hurt, I can cause you serious pain."

She went into the bathroom while the three of them laughed. Stupid men. What the hell did they think they were going to do, sit on her? Tie her to the bed? The police had just cleared her, and she wasn't going to waste another minute screwing around there.

She came out of the bathroom a few minutes later to get her clothes. The nurse said that she'd put them in the little cabinet by her bed, and she nearly screamed when the light came on, and Daniel was sitting in her bed...without his shirt, and if his pants lying over the chair were any indication, he wasn't wearing those either. She was going to go about her business as if he wasn't there.

"You can put them on you, but I'm going to simply take them off again. I think you should come here and save us both a great deal of energy and let me make love to you." She couldn't believe him and pulled her bag out of the cabinet without a word. "Too bad. I gave you the chance."

He pulled his cell out and pushed a button. She should have moved, but the door burst open, and three men walked in, each of them with vests on and headgear. She would have laughed that someone thought it'd take three men to do whatever they thought they were going to do to her but simply dropped her bag and picked her stance.

Chapter 10

"Well, find someone else. What the fuck did you do, find the first person you came across and hired her? Mother fuck. If she wasn't ready for us before, she certainly will be now." Berto wanted to throw his phone across the room but didn't want to go through the hassle of buying a new one and having it programmed. He didn't know a single number without the speed dial on the stupid thing. "Get someone in there now and kill the cunt. I want her dead."

"She's got someone in there with her at all times. And the way he took out the woman, the *trained* woman I had go into her room, means he's got some major training of his own. He took her out in less than a minute. With a bullet in his gut." He heard Jeannie laugh. "He sounds like someone you should hire on instead of having me kill."

Berto decided that as soon as this was over, Jeannie Whitney was dead. He didn't like that someone tried to tell him what to do, and even less that it was a woman. He took several deep breaths before he said something that they'd both regret.

"Where are you?" She told him that she was in Nashport, Ohio, in a little hotel outside of a smaller town called Dresden. "I'm coming there. Book me into something, and it had better be five-star, or I'm taking it out on your ass."

"Promises, promises," she said in that sultry voice that made his cock ache. "I don't know what you expect in the five-star range, but I'll see what I can do. There are a couple of bed and breakfasts that are nice. If you want something more, then you'll have to travel a ways. Columbus is the only place near here that has even a Radisson."

He told her to book the entire B&B and hung up on her. She'd either do it, or she'd be finished working for him a lot sooner than either of them expected. He called for his butler to get him a bag set up for several days and to get the jet ready. He hated to leave his hometown right now; there were many things going on that he should be overseeing, but this woman owed him. And he wanted to collect right now.

He picked up the picture of the woman. It was blurry, and he couldn't really make out more than it was a female, but it was the best that could be found of her. He tossed it on his desk with a snort. The stupid woman was harder to find than he was. He thought about taking lessons from her the next time the Feds went looking for him but decided he wouldn't stoop low enough to figure it out from a woman. Besides, she'd be dead in a few days, and then they'd be focusing on her and not him and the upcoming trial.

He was being indicted. Not unusual for someone in

the business like him, but still, it was something he didn't have time for. He had a shipment coming in on a ship in a few days, and having to leave now to go to Podunk, Ohio, wasn't what he wanted to do right now. Plus, there was the arsenal that was always waiting at the end of his private drive, ready to take him in if he so much as walked out of the gates. Fucking bastards.

Berto looked around his home. It was lavish and rich, not only in money but in things he'd "collected" over the years. Things that he'd wanted, and when he couldn't buy or steal, he'd simply claim. The house he was currently living in wasn't really his but had belonged to someone he'd killed for their territory last year. The idiot had stupidly decided that he wanted a bigger chunk of Berto's territory, and well…he'd objected. Quite harshly. His phone ringing again brought him to the present.

"Sir, the plane is on standby, and your luggage is on its way to the airstrip now. I have taken all the usual precautions and have alerted the guard. Will there be anything else you require?" Berto grinned. This was what paying for the best got you.

"Yes. I'd like for you to make sure that the household goes on as if I'm here." He didn't want his butler, whatever his name was, to think he had pegged his needs perfectly. "And I want you to make sure that when the vase comes in sometime over the next few days, I want to be notified immediately."

There was no vase. He just wanted to see how he would react to the news. The "very good, sir" was always the same answer, and he wondered if the man ever got ruffled or pissed. When he'd applied for the job, Berto had been hesitant. Now he wished he'd had him at every one of his homes.

The limo was at the front door when the door was opened for him, and Rogers—he remembered the butler's name now—had his coat and hat over his arms. He didn't register why he thought he'd need a hat and coat in Florida until he was zooming toward the runway. Laughing, he decided to give him a raise. The man was a genius to remind him gently that it was chilly where he was going.

They were speeding down the runway when his champagne was brought to him. Soon after they were in the air, three women came out of the backroom. Smiling, he thought about Rogers again. The man was definitely going to get a bonus for this. He lay back on the couch and let each of them take any part of him they wanted. He nearly came when one of them had his cock in her mouth before she even had him completely out of his trousers. Christ, this was going to be a relaxing trip, after all.

~~~

They stood there and waited. Doyle smiled when he heard the first crash. Then when something bumped hard against the door, he looked over at Royce. The man looked worried.

"She won't hurt them too badly. She knows not to kill them." Doyle didn't think he'd helped, especially when Royce took a step forward. "You go in there, and she'll flatten you, too."

"How do you know it's not her getting tossed around? What if they've gone overboard on what you told them to do?" He looked at the door again. "And how do you know that it's not Daniel throwing them around?"

"Because I trained her." He took pity on the man and walked to the door when it was finally quiet. "Look, if she's not hurt and still standing, I'll...I'll work for you for free for a whole six months. If she's down due to them and not because your brother has finally figured it out and took her to bed."

"Daniel and her?" Royce looked at the door and grinned. "Daniel can be very persuasive. You should see him in court."

Doyle didn't doubt it. But he also knew Dawn...Reilly. The woman had been obsessed with learning from him. And he'd been a very willing teacher. The girl...woman had a fire in her, a need. He only wished now that he'd taken the time to understand what drove her, rather than marvel at her ability to learn so well.

Doyle knocked on the door and laughed when he heard her ask if it was round two. "No, it's me. Can I come in without you kicking my ass, too, or should I send in Royce here to wear you down a bit more?"

When she didn't answer, he thought something was wrong and nearly went in anyway. But when she spoke, much closer to the door this time, he knew there was something else going on.

"Okay, but I didn't do anything to Mr. Hunter. One of the guys...well, he sort of hit him and knocked him over. I guess if he'd not been trying to help so much, I might have found a way to throw him somewhere else, but.... Is Royce going to be pissed?"

Doyle looked at the other man who was grinning and shaking his head. "No, he's okay with it. So long as Daniel isn't too badly hurt."

"Nah. He'll make it. Too bad, really." The door opened, and he looked at her. Not even a drop of sweat on her. "Those guys, however, won't be walking all that well for a few days. And that one," she kicked him in the ribs. "He doesn't play well with others. He needs to have his ass kicked again."

Doyle knew who the guy was and hadn't wanted to send him in with the other two. He tended to get a tad overzealous when he was doing hand-to-hand. Then Doyle thought maybe this was perfect. He laughed when he picked up a glass on her bedside and dumped it on the other two.

The room was a mess, and Daniel was just coming around. The man had a small bump on his head but no blood. Doyle thought he was lucky. Not many men or women came up on her without having more to show for it. When they got the men rounded up and on their feet, the younger one, Billy Shore, stuck out his hand to Reilly.

"I've been trained by the best, and you sure are fantastic. I'd like to have another go around with you sometime when you have—"

The low growl from across the room had all of them turning. Daniel Hunter had the look of a man who was having his favorite toy played with, and he'd never given permission. Reilly, of course, ignored him.

"I would love to have some fun sometime. I can't for a while yet. I have a big show coming up in another three weeks, and I want to get a few more pieces done for it. But I'll give you my number, and you can call me." She took the paper and pen he handed her and glared at the man who snatched it away.

"Get out of here now while you still can." The low words had the desired effect. All three men moved to the door as if a fire had been lit under their asses. When Daniel raised a brow to him and his brother, Royce laughed and went out, too. He stopped at the door before going out.

"You mind what you've been taught, little brother. Mom won't be happy if you aren't protecting her." He went out the door laughing. Doyle didn't move.

"The woman from this morning was found with a great deal of cash in her possession. We figure it was either from Carver or a jilted lover." He'd tried for a joke but failed miserably if Daniel's face was any indication. "There will be more attempts. And from my test just now, I know you can protect yourself and probably the kid, but it would help us a great deal if you told us what you think he wants from you. After four years, the man has a powerful hard on to get it back."

"I don't know. I swear to you, I don't know if it's not Benny." Doyle nodded. So she'd figured out it might not be the kid. But he had a feeling she might know more than she was letting on. "All I got from my sister was her things that the police sent me. And they were already packed up. They told me when they went to her home."

"Why don't you think it's Benny anymore?" They both looked at Daniel when he asked. "You seemed to think he's not it, why? There has to be something I missed. What is it? You? Does he want you?"

"As far as we can tell, it's not her. He seems to believe,

like most of the world, that O'Reilly Harlequin is a male. And for as long as you've been famous, he figures he's older. Much older." Doyle walked to the door as he finished up. "There'll be a guard posted outside this door twenty-four-seven, so I wouldn't plan on leaving tonight if I was you. Benny has a guard, too, at Curtis's home. And we have somebody watching both your houses. Carver will be on his way soon if he hasn't left already. So settle in and enjoy your evening."

Doyle's phone was ringing when he exited the room. He smiled when he heard Reilly start cussing, and laughed when he heard her calling Daniel a great many colorful names he'd never heard of before. Some of them in another language.

~~~

"He's on his way to Ohio. His plane left just over twenty minutes ago and will land in a little runway in Zanesville. There are trackers on his plane and on his luggage. Ping number to find him is being texted to you. I don't know where he's staying yet, but I'll give you that when I have it. Happy hunting."

The phone went dead. He knew that the next time his plant called, there would be only a message like this one and no conversation. He hoped that this person didn't ever get caught. It would be nice to have someone like this on the side of the Feds and not out there on their own.

His phone alerted him he had a text, and he read the numbers there. He'd have to get to his house to see what he could bring up with this frequency but wasn't worried. There wasn't any way Carver was getting away again. Doyle called his contact with the Feds he'd been using for a few weeks now.

"He's on his way. He's coming in somewhere in Virginia, I heard. You going to go with me there?" Doyle grinned a sardonic grin. He'd had this man pegged as the leak for months now. "I can be there in about two hours."

"Yeah, you go to Virginia, and I'll send a couple of men to meet you there. Meantime, I'm going to see if I can get in to see this girl again. She might know something she doesn't realize yet. I heard some bastard took out a shooter this morning. He must have some major balls."

Doyle turned around and headed back to Reilly's room. "Yeah, heard that. I'm leaving the hospital now. I only hope I can get there in time to stop this killer. He's been around long enough." Doyle opened the door to the room without knocking and looked wide-eyed at the couple breaking apart from what appeared to be a very heated kiss. "You sending over someone else to keep an eye on the girl, or should I get a couple of my guys to come in? The Hunter Corp has a big security firm."

"No. We don't want any civilians hurt. Just have the three there wait, and when I get there with a few more, we'll let them get home. They need to come in and write up a couple of reports anyway." He hung up a few seconds later.

Doyle closed his phone and looked at the couple. "Change of plans. We have to move now. You're going to be having visitors in about ten minutes, and I'd just as soon not have to explain why you're one kickass broad."

They were going out the drive in the ambulance as they watched three dark sedans pull into the parking garage.

Doyle watched the nine men go into the elevator they'd just come out of and laughed when the thing wouldn't close. He'd bought them about twenty minutes because now they'd have to walk up the stairs to the seventh floor and not ride. And once there, they'd spend a bit more time chasing her around the hospital as one department after another told them where they thought the girl had gone. He figured they had about two hours if they were lucky.

"They going to hurt anyone when they figure it out?" Doyle shook his head at her question. "Why are you so sure?"

"Because as of late last night there were more Feds in that hospital than staff. They know what's going down and who the second is. They'll only slow him down to give us time. As soon as the allotted time is up, they'll nail them all, and hopefully, someone sings before too much longer."

"Sings what?" Daniel asked as he held onto Reilly. The girl didn't seem to mind too much, but she still wasn't comfortable with him. Doyle hoped they'd work it out.

"Everything. Agent Patrick Snodgrass, my boss, when I asked to come back in just for this case, has been giving someone information for a few months. It wasn't until he let a little tidbit slip about six weeks ago that I figured out one of the people making it so he could afford those fancy cars and vacations was Carver. I just needed to connect the dots so everyone could see, too."

"So, you knew this guy was dirty when you came to work for me." Doyle nodded at Daniel's question. "Were you going to tell us about it before he killed someone in my family?"

"Your family was never in danger. Reilly here wasn't even his target until about six months ago. That's why I don't think it's the kid he's after. I'm not even sure he knows about him. There has to be something else."

Doyle waited, but nothing was coming. He had time, not a lot but a little time, for her to tell him. He was hoping she'd come forth with it if there was anything. He didn't come right out and ask her because he liked her and knew that if he accused her of something she'd clam up tight. He looked around when they pulled into the Harlequin compound. Holy shit, this woman was prepared, more so than he'd thought.

Chapter 11

He had to tell her. Benny had the backpack all ready to give her when she came in the door. He just didn't expect to see Daniel and the other men come in with her. He kicked the pack under the couch and went to give her a hug. Over the last few days, he'd come to enjoy her hugs and couldn't understand why he'd shied away from them before.

"I've been so worried. Curtis and his wife brought me over about two hours ago, it seems, and he said you'd be right along. I made us some dinner." He flushed. He sounded like some worrywart, and he wasn't really. "I guess we can get some more chicken out of the freezer."

"I won't be staying, but thanks. Kylie and I have to get home, she's not feeling well, and this far into her pregnancy is scary." Curtis ruffled his hair. "You're a good kid. I hope we get to see you for Thanksgiving this year."

Kylie kissed his forehead, and he flushed again. *Man, the women around here sure liked to suck face,* he thought. He wanted to ask to feel the baby again but was afraid to. But Kylie suddenly made a funny noise in the back of her throat and grabbed his hand.

"Wow." The way her belly rolled against his hand made him think it had to hurt her, but she had the weirdest look on her face like she thought it was a Christmas present or something. She held his hand there, and he wondered what it would be like to have a little brother or sister, and stiffened his shoulders. He had no mom, really, and he didn't think he'd ever want anything to do with who he thought was his sperm donor. He pulled his hand back slowly, and she smiled down at him.

After they left, Doyle and Daniel walked around the house for a bit, and he and Reilly finished up dinner. He was as ready as he'd ever be and started talking.

"I have that backpack in the living room, and I think I know why the man who calls you is trying to get it back. Mom gave it to me the day she got beat up and killed, and she told me it was my insurance. I didn't know what she meant, but I kept it safe like she said."

Reilly laid down her knife and sat in the chair. "Do you know what's in it?" He nodded. "Is it something bad, something that might get you into trouble if someone other than that man knew you had it?"

He wasn't sure. But he knew that lying to her would be worse than if he told her nothing. "I think so, but I don't know. There is…do you want it?"

She didn't answer, and when the men came back in the house, she looked at him again and shook her head a little. He nodded just as much and hoped that he understood her

111

that he wasn't to talk about it with them there. He helped her with dinner as everyone talked about nothing much of anything. After dinner, she asked him if he wanted her to walk with him. He nodded.

"I don't know what to say right now. Would you mind if I talked to Daniel about it?" He shook his head as she sat down on his bed. "Benny, I don't want anything to happen to you. I love you very much. I was afraid when you first came to me. I had no idea what I was doing. But we haven't done so bad, have we?"

"No. I know I've never said it to you, but I love you, too. And Reilly, you have given me a lot, too. My mom…she wasn't really very…she was…." He wiped at the tears that both embarrassed him and made him a little angry. "She wasn't always there, and when she was, she was doped up."

"I know. I know."

She held him for a little while. He was nearly asleep when he heard her sniffle. She'd been crying. Instead of talking to her or saying the wrong thing, he squeezed her. She returned his tight grip, and he pulled away.

"I won't let him hurt you, too. I promise you, he won't hurt you like he did, my mom." She nodded at him and looked away.

"I thought we should…you know, run, but I don't know. If we do, there might not be the same kind of…Daniel and the others, they've been very nice and supportive. Even…."

He waited, but when she didn't finish, he did. "Even though you've been a pain in the ass to them?"

"Funny." She tickled him. "I meant to say even though it's not their fight. But I don't…maybe it's better we stay and take a stand. Fight for us instead of running. We would have to run a long time if we started that now."

Benny rolled to his side when she kissed him again and left. He loved her very much and really didn't want anything to happen to her. And he really liked Daniel and his brothers. They were big and strong, and they ruffled his hair. He grinned. He didn't act like he liked that, but he did. And besides, their friend Willow said he could have a puppy of his own when her dog had her litter. Life wasn't so bad now, he figured.

~~~

Daniel was standing in the hall when O'Reilly came out of the bedroom nearest him. He wasn't sure what to make of the expression she had on her face, but he went to her to hold her. She stepped back, and he stopped.

"I need to talk to you when Doyle leaves. Is that all right?" She looked down the hall and then pointed to the room across from the one she'd come out of. "You can stay in here. There's a bath and plenty of towels if you need them."

Ignoring her reference to where she thought he was sleeping, he spoke. There was no way he wasn't going to be in her bed tonight. "Doyle said he'd bunk on the couch. You have cable and a big screen. I think he said something about some soccer games. Why don't we go to your room and we can talk."

She looked indecisive. He wasn't going to force her, but he did want her. When she nodded and turned to go down the hall, he followed her. He hadn't even realized there was a door down this far.

"I sleep in the basement. I have my own entrance, and I

can come and go when I need to be out in the shop without waking Benny. He knows that if he needs me, he can come out there or simply use the intercom. He's a really good kid. I don't want anything to happen to...I'm babbling."

The room that the short set of stairs led them to was massive. He could see that she'd done some extensive work on this end of the yard and house. The entire back end of her room opened up to a back patio that looked like it held a hot tub as well as a pool not far from where they stood. He walked over to the door and opened it. She rushed toward him and slid open a small panel and punched in a code.

"I don't want the police to come here again. The last time was a while ago, but they do test it every month." She slid the panel back. "You can go out and in now until the door closes. It'll alarm again once the door crosses the frame. It's automatically charged then."

She was so close, and before she could step back, he pulled her gently into his body. She stiffened slightly, then leaned into him. Daniel lifted her chin up so that her mouth was where he could enjoy it.

He was careful of her back and his side where he'd been shot. The area was aching right now, but there wasn't any way he was going to stop. When she moved her arms up to his shoulders, he put his hand on her hip and pulled her tight. He tasted her sigh when he rocked into her.

"I should tell you about...Benny and I talked.... Daniel, you should listen to me." He wanted to make her forget everything but him.

He lifted his hand from her hip and cupped her breast. Her nipple pebbled under his thumb. When he shifted her so that he could pull her over his thigh, she tightened around his leg.

Making love to her was going to be a challenge. He couldn't roll her to her back like he wanted to do to bury himself into her heat, and he didn't think he could lift her up and take her standing. Backing them to where he'd remembered the bed was, he nearly fell against it when his legs touched it.

Pulling back, he lifted her shirt over her head. Daniel never stopped looking at her, waiting for any sign that she wasn't ready for what he wanted. When she crossed her arms over her chest, he pulled them down and put them at her sides.

"Don't. Not with me. I want to look at you." Her bra wasn't one of those sexy little ones women he knew wore, but a white one that said *I'm for use, not to seduce.* He moved the straps down her shoulders as he continued. "Do you know how much I've wanted to do this? Every time I've been close enough to touch you. And the day you sicced your dogs on me? I nearly took you on the hood of my car."

"Dogs? I don't...the watchdogs. They aren't mine. I'd been babysitting them. They're mostly stupid and only know 'kill' and 'heel.' And they run at everything that runs from them. The owner came and got them that afternoon." He leaned into her cleavage and reached behind her to unsnap her bra. "Daniel, please listen to me."

"What is it, baby? If you want me to stop...." He licked along the curve of her breast before taking her bra off. "If you want me to stop...I can't remember what I'm supposed to say with something this deliciously sexy right here for the

115

taking."

"I'm not any good at sex." He cocked a brow at her statement. Before he could speak, she rushed on. "I'm a lousy lay, and I've never really understood the whole purpose for it. Sex, I mean. I don't understand the big deal or why grown adults would go out of their way to…. It's time-consuming, and it's sort of a disappointment."

"Really," he said, and she nodded. "Who told you that you were a lousy lay? An old boyfriend, maybe? An ex-lover? Or did you come to this ridiculous conclusion all on your own?"

"He said that I was not worth it. And he wasn't the only one…well, I guess he was. After word got around that I was so terrible at it, it was hard to get a date after that. Not that I wanted to. Once was enough for me." She looked up at him when he growled. "I'm not telling you this so you'll feel sorry for me. I've heard other women talk about how good Alden is in bed. I should have known better than to—"

He turned her around and pushed her down on the bed. She stared up at him as he paced in front of her. "Alden, who? And the reason I ask is because I'm going to hunt him down and cut his dick off and shove it up his ass for him." Her giggle startled him. "You should know that laughing at a man when his woman's virtue is at stake is a no-no."

"His last name is Warren, and I'm hardly a virgin. I've just never…enjoyed sex, not that I didn't have it. And Alden meant well…well, no, he didn't. He was mean, and he blabbed it all over campus." She crossed her arms over her naked breasts and distracted him for a second. But he laughed when she continued. "Of course, I didn't tell anyone

I thought his wiener was tiny and pencil-like."

Suddenly everything fell into place. He was in love with this woman. Terror poured over him. For only a split second, then everything he'd ever wanted was right there. Daniel moved to the bed again and asked her to move up it.

"I want you. More than I've ever wanted a woman before, but I don't want to hurt either of us. You'll have to do most of the work, I'm afraid until I can take you properly." She swallowed twice, and his cock jerked in his pants as he watched her breasts move. He crawled up the bed to settle between her feet. "I want to taste you first. Can you lay on your back, or do you need another position to not hurt?"

He reached up to her jeans and unsnapped them. While he waited for her answer, he moved them slowly down her hips. He kissed a path down her body with his mouth, kissing and nipping at her flesh. She was warm and tasted like home to him.

"I can…I can stay this way for a little bit. I've…Christ." He laved his tongue in her belly button before he sat up and pulled her jeans all the way off. She was soaking wet, her panties were wet at the place he wanted to be worse than anything.

"You don't look like you're going to be a lousy lay. As wet as you are, it looks to me like I can slide into you deep and pound you hard without hurting you." He slid his fingers up her right thigh, then over her mound lightly, then down the other thigh. She undulated up off the bed. "Has anyone drank from you, O'Reilly? Suckled from your pussy until you came?"

Her hoarse *no* had him move closer to her and rub his

cheek over her heat. She tangled her fingers into his hair as he traced his finger over the elastic of her panties. When he moved under them and pushed his fingers into her, she cried out, and he decided that he'd had enough teasing. He wanted her now.

Exquisite. He gathered as much of her juices on his tongue and pressed his finger into her. She was riding his mouth, moaning loudly and tightening her thighs around his head. Christ, he wanted to make her come, and when he ripped her panties off and opened her with his fingers, he took her clit into his mouth and nipped.

Her scream tore from her as she came. Copious amounts of her hot cream poured from her body, and he drank and lapped at as much as he could. While she was still writhing under him, he sat up and nearly went back to her pussy when she whimpered.

"Easy, baby. I need to undress." His pants and boxers came off as one, and he practically tore his shirt off. "I'm going to fuck you, love. I don't want to hurt you so—"

"Now. Please now. I need you right now." He could hear her need, see it on her face and her body. He nearly ripped the condom wrapper in two when he tore it with his teeth. Getting it on his cock was painful and oh so worth it to be buried deep inside of her. Moving back between her thighs, he held his cock at her entrance. When she rocked up and took the head of his cock inside of her, she came again. Daniel entered her hard.

He didn't move. If he did, he was coming. Her body didn't just hold him, but gripped him, milked him. He tried to move so that he wasn't going to hurt her, but she wrapped her legs around his thighs and rocked up. He was lost after that.

Her nipple fit into his mouth like it was made to be there. He tried not to pound into her, but being gentle, being easy wasn't going to happen. When she came again, this time biting his shoulder, she brought him with her. His cock felt as if it exploded inside of her as he came. He would swear for the rest of his life that he felt his cum come from his ears. His entire body felt drained.

He didn't drop onto her, though he didn't know how he managed not to. He rolled her with him and let her spread over him as he waited for his heart to either explode or calm. Right now, he wasn't counting on ever being calm again. He kissed her forehead when she pulled the blanket over them and closed his eyes. He heard her sigh heavily before her breathing evened out, and he knew she was asleep.

Daniel Hunter didn't want to be in love. But he was pretty sure he was. He hadn't wanted it to happen. Hell, he never thought it would. He'd kept his heart firmly behind a locked door for so long that he was sure the key was gone. And the bundle in his arms had not only found the key but had moved right into the space and made him see reason.

That didn't really change the fact that he wasn't going to marry her. Love her, yes, he had no problem with that. But he had been around enough of his buddies to know that love was a fleeting thing and rarely lasted as long as a car loan. He kissed her head again as he closed his eyes. He'd stay with her for as long as they both wanted, but he decided to make sure she knew that marriage wasn't going to ever happen. If that was what she wanted, they might as well part company now.

He rubbed the area over his heart. For some reason, that had hurt him, and he didn't want—no, he *refused*—to think of it as anything more than a twinge of something because he'd enjoyed her so much. Smiling into the darkness, he decided that was it. He'd miss her. Closing his eyes, he let sleep take him. They'd talk tomorrow, he thought.

Chapter 12

Reilly was in the kitchen making Benny breakfast when the phone rang. She'd already opened the gate for Royce Hunter when he told her that he needed to speak to her and Daniel. She didn't want to let him in, but she was pretty sure that whatever the man had to say was important to their well-being. She nearly had Benny answer it when Daniel came into the kitchen and picked up the receiver as if he lived there or something. She turned her back to him so that she wouldn't snap at him.

"Harlequin residence. How may I help you?" He looked at her sharply, then turned his back away. She could hear him mumbling, but not the words. When he turned back around, she knew it had been Carver.

"Benny, why don't you go to your room so your aunt and I can talk?" She bristled.

"He stays. And don't answer my phone again. This is still my house." She put pancakes on Benny's plate and moved to get him the bacon. "What did he say?"

"I don't think—"

"No, you don't get to think. You also don't get to make guesses, nor do you get to decide what my son hears and doesn't hear." She put the plate down on the table a little harder than she'd meant to. "What did he say?"

"He said that he'll get you soon. And after he's finished raping every orifice of your body, he's going to do the same to your husband, who he thinks I am by the way. After that, he's going to drag you behind—"

"That's enough," Royce said. She looked over at Royce, and another man she'd never met before they entered the kitchen. Royce looked at Benny and jerked his head toward the other room. "Go in there and finish eating. You," he pointed to Daniel, "go outside."

"Fuck you. This is between her and I. And you will not—"

"Someone tried to kill Doyle last night," the other man said as he sat down. "He called me to tell me he was going to his apartment to pick up some clothes. Told me that he'd be back in an hour, that you and the girl here were in bed together." The man winked at her when he turned to her. "We both figured that you'd be safe enough. When I didn't hear from him this morning, I went by his place to see. He had been...he was hurt badly, and this was on his body. I'm pretty sure that whoever did it to him thinks he was left for dead. And the paper is going to confirm that fact."

Reilly found herself in a chair with her head between her knees. She didn't even fight the person holding her there. Her friend had been hurt because of her. She didn't listen to the men talking. She had enough in her heart right now to wonder if they were blaming her or not. It wasn't until she heard Benny's voice that she pushed against the hand holding her down and sat up.

"I think he wants this." Benny dropped the backpack on the table but didn't let it go. "My mom, my other mom, gave it to me when we saw those men pull up in front of the house. She told me to keep it safe, that it would be my insurance. I still don't know what that means, but it has stuff in there that he probably doesn't want people to know. And the money."

"Have you counted it, Benny?" The stranger got up and pulled a sheet of paper off her notepad, and grabbed a pen. "Tell me what they looked like, how many there were, and anything you can remember about that—"

"Excuse me, but who the hell are you? And what the hell are you doing in my...what the hell are any of you doing in my house? I think it's time you leave. I've got enough going on right now, and entertaining a bunch of wannabe cops in my kitchen isn't happening."

"I'm Agent Alan Levy with the FBI. I've sort of...I became friends of the family when Joey, Jesse's wife, had some issues with another bad guy. I'm here to help."

"I see. Actually, I don't." She stood up. "Thanks for your time, Agent, but you can take that bag with you when you leave. I don't care what's in it or what happens to it. As far as I'm concerned, Benny and I are going to start over today. Nothing happened before this morning."

"We slept together last night, and as far as I'm concerned, that *does* change things." Daniel stalked toward her. "You

123

aren't going to be doing this on your own anymore. Not now that I'm a part of your life."

"A part of my life? How do you figure that came about? I do not need a man coming into my home and acting like one night of fucking is going to get him whatever he wants." She flushed when one of the men cleared his throat. "I think it's time you all left. I have things to do today."

The agent sat down first, and then Royce. Reilly was ready to stomp her foot at them when Daniel sat as well. She looked over at Benny, who was trying his best not to laugh. She had no idea what he might have thought was funny about this whole thing, but she'd had enough. She was out the door and running across the yard when she heard cursing behind her. When she was grabbed and jerked around, she acted without thought.

Daniel was over her shoulder and flat on his back when she straddled him. He grabbed for her hands just as she doubled up her fist to hit him. Jerking free, she hit him twice in the face and was trying for another hit when someone knocked her off him and held her down. It took her a minute or two before she realized it was the agent.

"You hear me? Listen to me, Reilly, he's not going to hurt you." He shook her. "Damn it, woman, who the fuck trained you?"

"Doyle. Get off me. I want to get up." He stared down at her for several seconds before he spoke.

"Are you going to hit either of us?" She shook her head. "Okay. I'll let you up, but I'm not going to let you hurt me like he did."

She thought he was trying to make a joke but didn't get

it until he moved off her and she sat up. She'd hurt Daniel badly. She didn't want to feel bad for it, but she did. In fact, the tears were burning her eyes even as she got up to go to him.

"Are you all right?" he asked her. "I'm sorry I hurt you. I didn't mean to. I was only trying to protect you." He rubbed his jaw and wiped at the blood on his nose. "But I guess you can do that all on your own."

She dropped to her knees in front of him and let the tears fall. "He trained me to protect and not think. He said that thinking would get me killed. I didn't mean to hurt you."

"Yes, you did. But I deserved it." He cupped the back of her head and pulled her forehead to his. "O'Reilly, I don't want anything to happen to you or Benny."

She nodded, the only thing she could do around the lump in her throat. Here was a man willing to get the shit beat out of him by a woman and still not get pissy with her. She lifted his chin up when he let her go to look at his face.

"I think I broke your nose. And you're going to have a hell of a shiner tomorrow." She grinned. "And Royce is probably going to tell everyone I did it."

She stood up when he did and winced at the pain. She could feel the burn at her back, hurting now, and she looked at his side to see that he was bleeding there as well. She started to ask him if he needed to go to the doctor but didn't get the chance when he pulled her to him and kissed her.

It wasn't near long enough, his tongue only brushing over hers for a second. His hand cupped her hip, but he didn't pull her close. When he pulled his mouth from hers, she looked up at him and could see more than pain in his eyes.

"We aren't finished. We have something starting here, and I don't want it to end. I can't do permanent, never will actually, but we can have some fun, right?" She put her head on his shoulder to hide her pain. She nodded, and he sighed. "I knew that you'd understand. Marriage is fine for some, but I'm not one of those kind of men. I never want to be in a relationship that has bonds that tie us together."

She was saved from making a fool of herself when Alan cleared his throat again. "I'd like to see what's in that backpack now. To see if whatever's in it was worth a good man's life."

She stepped from Daniel and went to the house. Royce was standing on her deck with Benny, and he held the backpack like it was a part of him. She ruffled his hair as she went by and laughed when he said the pancakes were cold now.

"I'll make some more. You go ahead and give them everything you have. I want this over with so that you and I can move on, okay?" He nodded but looked at Daniel, who was still in the yard with Alan. "He's not going to be here much longer, I think. Just you and me, kid."

Reilly went into the house and started a new batch of batter. Her heart hurt so much that she wanted to find a dark corner and cry. She'd done something incredibly stupid. She'd fallen for a man, finally, who only wanted a good roll in the sack and no attachments.

~~~

Royce knew that his brother had hurt Reilly. He wasn't sure what he'd said, but he had an idea. Daniel had been saying that marriage wasn't for him for nearly all his life. The girl looked to be about in love with his stupid brother, and he had no idea how to tell her he could be changed. Or that he'd be worth it if she tried.

When Daniel came into the house, Reilly had just set a platter of pancakes in front of him. He was scooping off several of them when a plate of sausage was put next to him. Damn, but he was starved. He watched her put more sausage and also bacon in a pan. He got up to get more plates and glasses while chewing the best pancakes he'd ever eaten. Daniel simply paced the room.

"Can I help you?" Benny asked. Daniel looked down at him. The kid looked a lot like Carver and nothing like the woman who he now called Mom. He wondered what his real mother looked like. "Reilly lets me get the stuff to put on them. And I have to clear and wash if she cooks."

"You cook?" Royce asked, and Benny nodded. "My wife can't cook. She's really terrible at it, but she tries. She's better at ordering out than in. I cook some, but we have a live-in cook that does a fantastic job. But if you tell anyone I said that, I'll...." He didn't want to say *beat you*. He'd seen the pictures of his mom. "I'll tickle you until you scream like a little girl."

"Reilly said that I might meet somebody someday who couldn't, and eating out wasn't healthy. I like to do it. I'm not as good as she is, but I can do pretty good."

Royce had no doubt. He nodded and handed him a stack of plates as he gathered up some silverware. His phone ringing made him jump. It had been a hell of a morning so far.

"I'm thinking that staying here since he knows you live here is a bad idea. I think you should move in with me. I have a security system and—" Daniel snapped his mouth closed when O'Reilly cut him off. Royce was going to love this girl.

"No. Benny and I are staying here. I want you people to see what's in that bag and get that thing out of my house." She stood up to get herself another glass and sat down before continuing. "We have the best security system money could buy, an electrified fence surrounding the property, and I have to work."

"You don't know what you're dealing with here. He's a very—"

"I know exactly what I'm dealing with here." Her voice was calm as she spoke and put butter on her own stack of pancakes. "I saw firsthand what he's capable of. You, Mr. Daniel Hunter, are a pain in the ass." Royce stood when she finished eating and stood up. This time he was positive that she was going to brain his brother. "I have to go to work. Don't come out to the studio unless you're on fire."

When Daniel started to stand to no doubt go after her, Royce stopped him. "You might want to wait until she cools off a little bit. She's mad enough right now to cut you to ribbons and not give a fig about it."

"One time, I made her mad. She was okay when she came back into the house. Mr. Royce is right, leave her be. I swear she won't ground you as bad if you do." Royce wanted to laugh at Benny's serious tone but was worried he'd hurt the boy's feelings. "I'm going to do the dishes while you guys ask me what you want. I can...I like to keep my hands busy when I'm nervous."

They all put their dishes on the sink, and Benny washed the table down for them. He asked if they needed any more to drink, then filled the sink. Alan picked up the bag and put it on the cleared table. The zipper opening was loud in the otherwise silent room.

Alan looked poleaxed when he looked inside. Royce had already figured there was money, but not how much. A lot was all he could think of. Benny's mother had had plenty of time to gather it, but the bag, while the biggest one he'd ever seen, still probably didn't hold all that much.

He was wrong.

He'd never thought of the denomination of the money. He'd been thinking small time. Meagen had not. The money, now dumped on the table, was over five million dollars, Royce thought. Alan picked up one of the stacks and fanned it.

"It's real. And there's nearly...." He started staking the money in piles. "There's close to fifteen, maybe as much as twenty mill here." Alan picked up one stack and nodded to Benny, who still had his back to them. "Benny, did you ever spend any of this? On anything?"

"No, sir. Reilly gave me all I ever needed. Sometimes when I really wanted something, she'd make me work it off, but I never once thought of spending it. She's been really great to me. I was keeping it because...." He didn't turn, but his shoulder tensed up. "In case she didn't want me anymore."

"She'd never do that, buddy. She loves you very much." Royce looked at Daniel when he spoke and wondered how much he loved the boy. "She'd cut off her right arm before she'd let anything happen to you."

"I know that now, but back then…not so much." Benny turned to face them. "She's going to get hurt 'cause of me, huh?"

"Not if I can help it." Daniel told him. "Not even if I have to tie her to the bed to keep her safe."

"No. She can get away. That man, he showed her how to get out of that, too. He taught her how to do all kinds of cool stuff. Me, too, when I got older. He's a scary nice man."

Royce was glad to see that Reilly had not been hiding behind the gated house she lived in and had also made her nephew aware as well. The man they were afraid of wasn't going to give up until he got whatever it was he came for. But Benny spoke again, and Royce felt the hair on his neck dance.

"There's ledgers in the front pockets. Ten, I guess. It's got names and dates in it, along with other stuff. I think they're favors that that man did for those people. Might even be some dead guys in it." He flushed before turning around to the sink again. "I looked at those things. A lot of the people in the red one are dead. Some of them are marked off, but…well, I have a list like that, too, and I've marked off the ones that weren't marked yet."

Royce looked over at Alan, who was looking at the ten colored composition notebooks that had been in the front pocket. They were colored and labeled. The only red one was marked simply "GONE." Royce picked that one up.

Name after name was in there. The ones that had a single penned line through it were followed by a date. There was also a number. It wasn't until Daniel laid out a map that he realized what they meant. They were places that coincided with the names in his book. And Royce would bet his last dollar if they went there they'd find those people buried there.

"He's keeping track of where they are so that he won't… visit the same place twice." Royce nodded at Daniel's comment. "There are over two hundred numbers on this map. You think he killed that many people?"

"Or had them killed." Alan handed them one of the ledgers opened to a page and pointed. "The police department and their names. All of them it seems, from the chief to the desk clerks. There are even references to some of the biggest trials in the state here."

"He's going to come after that, I know it. And it's not me like you all think. Mom made sure he didn't know about me. He thinks she had an abortion." Benny turned and hung the towel he'd dried his hands with on the sink. "I think I'd like to go out to Reilly now. Don't come out, 'cause she'll get mad again, but I need to be with her. When you go out, the code is twenty-four seventy-nine. It's a onetime code, so when you leave, the gate will be on fry again. Good-bye."

He moved out the door without another word. Royce looked over at his brother, then at Alan. This was much more serious than any of them had thought. And if Alan's face was any indication, he was thinking the same thing.

Chapter 13

Berto was settled in the bed and breakfast when he suddenly knew he wasn't alone. He didn't jump, as he was sure the woman thought he should have, but looked at her over his newspaper, all ten pages of it.

"I thought you'd like it here better than the other one. This one at least has separate bathrooms." She sat on his bed without his permission. When she started to take off her blouse, his cock jerked. "Wanna fuck around while we wait on the guys I have watching the estate to call in?"

Hell yes, he did, but he wasn't going to do what she wanted. He had a fleeting thought to have her undress to see if she was wearing a wire, but he knew that if he had her naked, he'd be bending her over the bed and losing himself deep inside of her. He didn't want her to win.

"No, I do not. And this place is a hovel. Why didn't you simply purchase a house for us to use instead of renting a room here?" He was lying and was pretty sure she knew it.

He waited for her answer, and when none was forthcoming, he asked again.

"And just where was I supposed to get a bank loan to purchase a house? This is Sunday, and when you called me yesterday—"

He slapped her. When she tumbled off the bed, he saw that her skirt had ridden up her thigh, and she wasn't wearing anything under it. This time his cock ached so badly that he nearly doubled over from it. The plane ride yesterday with the three women didn't even take the edge off when it came to fucking this woman. She liked it as rough and hard as he did. He turned his back on her and went to his chair again.

"Don't fuck with me, Jeannie. I told you I wasn't in the mood. Now. When I ask you a question, I expect answers, not smart-assed replies that have nothing to do with it." He picked up the file he'd brought with him. "That girl you hired, she was a waste. All she did was get in the room and get off a shot before that Hunter man killed her. I want to know why you picked someone so incompetent, and what the fuck do I need you for if that's the type of help you find for me?"

He watched her stand up. There was blood on her blouse, and her lip was swollen. She sat on the bed and straightened her clothes before she answered. He knew she was stalling either from anger or trying to come up with a good answer. He waited, giving her time. He could always tell when someone was lying.

"Actually, I didn't find her. Your boy did." He frowned. Boy? But she cleared up his confusion by continuing. "Micky found her. She was already in place by the time I got here. I never said anything because I know how useful he is under normal circumstances." She shrugged.

"Micky was supposed to find out information about her, not set her up to be killed." He realized then that the other man hadn't come to him even though he was pretty sure he knew he was in this town. "Where is he?"

"Don't know. Last I heard from him was when I came here. He met me at the airport, gave me a rundown of what was going on, and then...." She shrugged again. "I never had any contact with him. He might have realized what he'd done to fuck up and left town. Or could be he is hiding here."

"Find him. I want to know where he is right fucking now." He stood up and tossed the paper on the floor. "That Harlequin guy is having a show in four days. He'll come out for it and bring that bitch of a wife of his with him. I plan on being there when he does. His little missus is going to be a great deal of fun and as dead as her sister when I'm finished with her."

"It says here that it's by invitation only. Want me to get you a ticket?" He'd already checked on that and found that it was sold out. He'd crash it if he had to, but let her try. "How many do you need, and what do you want as backup?"

"Two, you and I will go as a couple and a limo with a driver that's mine. You might want to see about getting something suitable to wear. Nothing that is going to bring attention to us, so leave your nipples covered up."

She nodded and left soon after. He thought about fucking her anyway but decided that next time she'd be less likely to make a pass. Then he'd take her hard and fast, satisfying only himself. Berto pulled out the second file he'd brought with him. This one was on the kid he'd not known about.

The staties here weren't as helpful as the ones he had on his payroll back in Florida. He hated that he couldn't simply call his cops up and get what he needed, but the boys in blue here were a little more closed mouthed. All he'd been able to glean from the search of the courthouse was that O'Reilly had a son and that there had been nothing else about him. He didn't go to public schools, he didn't drive, nor did the little cock sucker have a birth certificate in this state. And he wasn't paying two hundred bucks to find out where he'd been spawned at. But Berto did have something else he could use against the woman if she didn't give up what he wanted.

He needed those ledgers. The money would be nice to have to run with, but not necessary. Berto knew that he had accounts all over the world and only needed to pick up another one of his passports to get to it. But the ledgers would get him killed in any number of ways. And not just by the Feds.

He hadn't made it to the top of the most wanted list by being polite and asking for territories. He'd been ruthless and cold; he'd murdered, raped, and lied himself into his position, and he wasn't going to lose it over a piece of ass.

How she'd gotten the ledgers out of his safe was still a mystery to him, and he'd never gotten an answer about where the money was from her no matter how much he'd hurt her. He looked down at the bite mark on his hand and got pissed all over again. She'd bitten him that day, and the fucking cunt had spit her blood in his face, too. He'd lost it then. He'd thought he'd ended her life, but all he'd done was make his life more difficult. His phone ringing startled him, and he looked around the room to see who'd seen him jump before he picked it up. It had been over an hour since Jeannie had left.

"He's in the morgue. I'm going to see if I can go in and make sure in an hour. I'm going in to see if he's my long lost brother." Jeannie laughed. "I'll see if they let me take a pic of him to send to you, too."

She was still laughing when she hung up. He decided the next time she came to him, he was killing her. She was getting much too comfy in her position. He wondered again if she wore a wire and shook his head. No, not her. He had a file on all that she'd done for him, too. Smiling, he thought about having her in his bed one last time. He was going to literally fuck her to death.

~~~

Daniel went out to the studio. He'd not been there yet, so when Benny told him that he could probably see her and not get hurt, he left the house. It had been several hours since his brother and Alan had left, and he wanted to see her.

The door wasn't locked, but Benny had told him it wouldn't be. She left it open when she was working in the event he might need her. She wasn't in the first room he went into and looked around before moving on.

This room looked like a storage room. There were stacks of wood in varying sizes and a nail gun hanging from the ceiling on one side of the room. Pictures hung here and there. He didn't read what they were about but walked around more. A large roll of bubble wrap hung from the ceiling on the other side, and a pallet of cardboard that looked like boxes. They were stamped with a large H in the middle and a smaller O and D on either side of it. Her logo.

There was a laptop, as well as a small printer, a large scale, and a long desk. He figured this was her shipping department and wondered if she had someone do it for her. He knew that she wouldn't trust anyone to do this for her and moved through the doorway into a larger room.

She was at the far end, sitting at a wheel. He'd tried to take a pottery class while he'd been in college and decided that it wasn't for him. He quietly watched her as she centered a pot. She was perhaps fifty feet from him, and when she glanced up at him, she didn't seem surprised. She answered his unspoken question before he could ask her if Benny had called her.

"I have an alarm on the door. Benny knows to reset it, but he hadn't told you when he okayed you coming here. He let me know you were coming and not to shoot you if the alarm sounded."

He'd have to remember to thank the kid when he went back to the house. "He said that you'd probably be over the worst part of you being pissed at me, and I could chance it. I thought coming down here, and groveling might help me get into your good graces again."

"Doubtful. I have some work to do. What do you want?" He wasn't discouraged. Much. "Tell me you're taking the bag and Benny and that I have seen the last of you and your family."

He moved further into the room. Now he was discouraged. He stood close enough to watch her pull the pot up but not close enough to let her hit him. That's when he noticed the gun in the chair behind her.

"Would you have shot me?" He wasn't thrilled when she continued to work with the clay and not answer him. He sat on the only other chair in the room. "I need to tell you how sorry I am. And to tell you that I was an ass."

She pulled the pot up to about a foot, then stopped the wheel and looked at him. "Yes, you are. Which time are you talking about? You know I don't care. I think it's been fun, but I don't really have time for this." She got up from the wheel and picked up the large cylinder.

There were nine of them on the shelves where she was taking this one. He noticed immediately that they were all the exact same height, and he noticed that they were in varying widths. He remembered the drawing she'd made for him.

It had been a tall vase, reaching nearly halfway up the stairs to the second landing. It had been fashioned into a water fountain that water came from the top and fell to a pool below it. He still didn't have a clue how she planned to make that work, but he knew that the vase had been small at the middle while the top and bottom had been tapered out and then flared at the top. He looked at the pieces and could almost see how she'd fit them together.

"Have you approved the colors yet?" He looked over at her when she spoke. "Mrs. Hunter, the one that owns the plant shop, said she'd send them to you to approve. I was wondering if you had an opportunity to see if they suited yet."

He sort of remembered an email from Joey, but for the

life of him couldn't remember what it had been about. There had been a mention of plants of some sort, but since he had no clue, he simply told her to use what she thought was right.

"She sent me a list of them with the colors. I think they'll be fine. When do you put this together?" She moved to the double sink near the far wall. He noticed that her gun was now in the back of her pants. "Are you planning to kill someone?"

"If they invade my turf, yes, I am. I'll have it in the kiln to bisque next week. Then the week after, I'll have most of the smaller pieces glazed together so that when I fire them again, it should be fine."

He saw several small pieces where she was headed with the moving cart and followed. When she moved a sheet of plastic out of the way, he could see that she had a drawing in much more detail than the one she'd given him hung on the wall. He looked at it in awe. If this was what she was doing for him, he was getting his money's worth. When she stood beside him, he looked at her and smiled.

"This is magnificent. I love it." He looked at it again, trying to see it the way his customers would. "I think they'll love it. It'll be calming and soft with the waterfalls, won't it? And the colors are perfect for the colors in the room where we want it."

"The fountain fixtures will be delivered first. I've already spoken to Stone Construction, and they said that they'd put it in for me. Apparently, they had put in the specs for this kind of thing while it was being built. And because the buyer backed out, they simple hid the main fixtures in the stairwell." She pulled out a pad of paper. "That will lower your bid. I hadn't realized that we'd not be starting from scratch."

He took the paper from her without seeing it. He dropped it on the floor and reached for her. When she tried to step back, everything in him wanted to snarl at her. Instead, he wrapped his hand around her neck and pulled her to him.

"Please, we can't do this anymore. Don't you see?" He could see, but not what she thought he should.

Daniel lowered his mouth to hers slowly. He wasn't sure what he was waiting for, but he knew when she gave it to him, he'd know. When her wet tongue came out and licked at her lush lips, he groaned. Something inside of him leaped for joy, and he took her mouth under his.

He couldn't get close enough standing the way that they were. He moved forward, moving her back and toward something, anything, that would bring her closer to him. When she stopped suddenly, he reached his hand out and touched the wall. *Yes*, his mind and body screamed. When she wrapped her fingers into his hair, he remembered the gun.

"Take it off. The gun," he growled at her. "Please. I don't want to accidentally shoot us when I strip you down to nothing and take you right here."

The loud thump gave him permission. He cupped her ass, and her legs wrapped around him. He rocked into her heat, knowing that when they came together, it wasn't going to be the soft lovemaking that he'd hoped for, but fast, dirty, and oh so sweet.

Daniel lifted her shirt and took her nipple into his mouth

before her head was free. He lifted the heavy flesh so that her nipple slid up from her bra, and he took it as deep as he could into his mouth. More, he needed more, much more.

Reaching to her back, careful even in his need not to hurt her burn, he ripped the soft lace free, never letting go of her hard peak. When she cried out, he knew it wasn't from pain but from a need as dark and primal as his was. Sliding his hands down the back of her jeans, he met with hot, hard muscles.

Turning around to look where he could go, he spotted a sturdy table. Without letting her go, he turned them both toward it while she tore at his shirt. He wanted to tell her she was killing him. But he couldn't think whether he wanted her to hurry or slow down. When he sat her ass on the table, he stepped back and looked at her.

"Christ, you're beautiful." And she was. Breasts heaving, nipple hard, and pink from his mouth. Her jeans were open, and he could see that she had on a pair of bright red panties. He wanted them off of her almost as much as he wanted to see her in nothing but them. When her foot reached out and ran up his cock, he grabbed the top of her jeans and pulled them off her, panties and all.

She was wet; her curls glistened in the light. Watching her face, he unsnapped his pants and slowly lowered the zipper. His cock was hurting, but the look on her face made it so worth it.

"I'm going to fuck you right here. Then when we're finished, I'm going to take you again in your bed. Then your shower. Then maybe the kitchen." He lowered his pants and moaned when she opened her legs for him. "You're going to tease me? A man on the edge?"

"Fuck me, Daniel. Take me right now, and stop fucking talking about it." She ran her fingers over her curls and then slowly entered her pussy. "Or I do it without you. Either way, I'm going to come."

He wrapped his hand around his cock and took the two steps to her. She put her feet in his waist and then around him when he stepped closer. There wasn't anywhere for him to go but deep inside of her when she pulled him to her using her feet. She cried out and lay back on the table, spread before him like a banquet.

He didn't move when he was seated in her. He knew that if he did, he was a goner. He let her ride him, doing all the work while he tried his best to regain control of himself. When she leaned up and took his mouth, Daniel slid out to his tip, then slowly lifted her off the table.

He lifted her up and down his cock, and every time her breast got within reach of his mouth, he took a nip. He knew she was getting close; her sheath was milking him hard. He put her back on the table and leaned over her, cupping both her breasts together until her nipples were only an inch apart. Taking them one at a time, sucking hard on them for several seconds, then going to the other, he pumped in and out of her.

"Come for me, O'Reilly. Milk my cock and bring me with you. Scream out my name and show me how much you love what I'm doing to you." Her entire body stiffened, and pain screamed along his cock, pleasure, and pain.

When she came, he showed no mercy. Pistoning in and out of her, he felt his own climax coming quickly. Before he could tell her to come again, she threw back her head and shouted that she loved him. Before he could ponder whether she meant what he was doing to her or that she actually loved him, Daniel came. Came hard, and again his entire body felt it. This time when he came, however, he felt the room darken around him and shift. It was several seconds before things righted themselves for him.

Chapter 14

Jeannie tried the number again. Still going straight to voicemail. She tossed the phone to the bed and glared at it. If she didn't reach her contact soon, she knew what she had to do. Kill Berto, then, come in, hoping that her other end knew enough to tell everyone she was one of the good guys.

"Ring, you stupid piece of shit." She nearly screamed when it did. Slowly picking it up, she didn't say anything after she clicked the button to start the call.

"I don't know who this is," said a male voice on the other end. "I know who this phone belonged to, but he can't come to it. He's been put to pasture." Jeannie closed her eyes and dropped on the bed. "If you'd like to leave a message now, I'll hang up and—"

"How? How did he...who put him to pasture?" She knew what that had meant. Her contact, after all this time, was brought in and was now deeply hidden within some cell. Which agency had pulled him was anyone's guess.

"I did." The pause was long enough that she knew he was waiting for the right response. Her problem wasn't that she didn't know what to say to him, but if she should. "I'm giving you fifteen more seconds."

"Undercover Agent Jeannie Whitney, special forces, FDA. I'm working with Agent Doyle O'Donnell, Retired." She took a deep breath and waited. She'd either just killed herself and her contact if he wasn't already dead or she had her new contact.

"Are you all right, Agent Whitney?" The question startled her. She'd been undercover for nearly three years, and she could say with all honesty that no one had asked her that before. "Are you coming in?"

"I'm…is Doyle all right? I didn't hear from him, and I…. No, I'm not coming in yet. My target is moving in on the woman. She has something he wants. A ledger, I think. Not sure what it has in it, but I hear things when I'm with him." She didn't have to tell him it was pillow talk; he had to know who she was and her jacket.

"I have the ledger. I'm not…let's just say that you're going to be safer with that sadist than coming in right now. O'Donnell was shot two nights ago. I had been going to meet him at his home when someone sprayed his house with bullets. Had I not been as close as I was, he'd be in the pasture, not out to it."

"You think it was inside." Not a question, but he answered anyway that he did. "It had to be someone higher up, I'm thinking. He told me the last time we talked that he thought it was Snot-ass…Snodgrass, Agent Patrick Snodgrass" She closed her eyes when he laughed. So much for being PC.

145

"I know about him. Doyle told me he thought he would try to take him out soon. We just didn't know it would be that night." She heard him sigh. "You tell me what you need, and it's yours. But this is the only phone I want you to use. If Carver is aware of you at any time, you drop and roll, understand?"

She was to disappear. Simply drop whatever she was doing and hide. But she had news for him, she was going to take the bastard out if it was the last thing she did. She agreed, but she thought he knew what she was planning.

"Don't go to the house. If you have a safe house, go there, but keep this phone with you. I'll need to bring you in when things go south." She hoped she could come in, but if Snot-ass knew about her, she wondered if Carver might as well. The man on the other end of the line answered her question before she could voice it. "Snot-ass, as you call him, believes you to be dead. I think Doyle had something to do with that. He made sure there are no pictures of you or any prints on file. I have that, as well. I've got your ass."

"You'd better." She told him when she realized how much this guy actually knew. "If you don't, I'm going to find your ass and give you a new orifice to shit from." His laughter did nothing to ease her anger. "You think I'm kidding, big boy?"

"Nope," he told her with humor. "I was just thinking I can't wait to meet you. Keep it high and tight, girl, and we'll get through this."

The line went dead, and she closed the phone. High and tight? What the fuck was that supposed to mean? And then she laughed. She had no idea who she'd just been assigned to.

Jeannie went to her "insurance" and pulled it out. There was more than enough money there to get her a fresh start, and she was tempted to just say fuck it all and do it. Putting the bag back under the floorboard, along with the phone that she plugged into the hidden outlet, she knew she couldn't do it. She was in too deep and had lost way too much.

Jeannie had been put into this position because she had the right looks, the right qualifications, as well as the balls to tell them she could do it. Now all this time later, she was still in, scarred more than she'd ever thought possible, and she was pretty sure that she'd be finished when they did manage to bring her in. As an agent, she knew that time out like she had been was not good on the old noggin. She'd been under longer than she'd been an agent, and would more than likely have to be retrained or killed.

She lay on the bed and thought of her next move. Carver was in the same town as the girl. Jeannie was only a few miles from them both in either direction. She was tempted to go to the girl and help her stand her ground. But if Carver got through and he found out what she had been doing, her entire life would be spent looking over her shoulder to see if he'd finally found her.

When her phone rang next to her bed, she let it ring once more before switching on the recorder and picking up the receiver. She put as much sleepiness in her voice as she could. Jeannie knew who it was. Carver and Micky were the only two with this number, and Micky, thanks to her, wasn't going to be calling her anytime soon.

"What did you find out about Micky? Is he a stiff, or was

it not your long lost brother?" She heard a car horn honk and then the hum of a window. He was riding somewhere.

"It was him. I tried to reach you to let you know, but it went to voice. I don't do voice for anything." She'd told him that before, and it was a lie. She just didn't leave a voicemail for him because she knew it irritated him. "You getting some on the side?"

She hoped so. Christ, she hated that part of her job. She'd love to meet somebody someday who wanted to have normal everyday kind of sex. Not the type where if blood was shed, all the better. As soon as this was over, she was going to take a bath for a week and scrub him off her.

"No, I was not. I've been tracking that girl. That potter has her tightened up so much I'm beginning to think there is no girl. And did you know there was a kid? She can't be as young as we thought if she has a kid in high school."

Fuck, he knows about the boy. Not, apparently, that it was his son, but he would only have to see the kid to figure that out. She didn't comment on the kid but snorted her answer. She had to get word to someone that he knew about the boy so they'd be extra careful about him being out. Not that Harlequin wasn't already doing enough of that, Jeannie thought. She'd done a hell of a job keeping him under wraps so far. His snapping made her realize that she'd missed something.

"Are you fucking sleeping again? Mother fuck. When I get my hands on—"

"I'm here. Damn it, I've been sick. I told you that I was seeing a doc about my back." Micky had returned fire and had nicked her in the shoulder. "What the fuck am I supposed to do when the pain shit makes me like a zombie?"

"I suggest you stop taking it and pay attention. I want you to scare her out. The girl or the boy, I don't care which. Because I figure like most 'mommies,' she's going to come running when he's been snatched up. Then bring the bitch to me, and I'll get my shit and leave this God forsaken fucking town."

She told him that she'd have him something by noon tomorrow. She hung up her phone and thought about what she needed to do. The girl was safe where she was, but it wouldn't take him long to figure out that she went out to the school at the Foundation once a day. It had been much too easy to get her schedule and know where she was going to be at all times. Jeannie got up and pulled out a few sheets of paper. Time to make plans. She just hoped that they weren't going to be the last ones she ever made.

~~~

Reilly walked around the huge classroom and watched each of the students she had try to center a pot. All of them had had some basics before coming here, but not many of them had actually been at a wheel. She'd been having a few problems with this one particular girl. Nothing she couldn't handle, but it was getting on her last nerve. Reilly glanced over at the door when someone knocked and walked in. Great. Another Hunter.

Mrs. Hunter, the elder, wasn't too bad. She had a sharp tongue and a sharper mind. Reilly doubted much got by her, especially concerning her sons. Reilly had learned earlier that morning that talking straight with the older woman threw her off her game, and she didn't hang around much.

When she sat at the small table they'd used to weigh up clay balls, she looked over at Benny, and he winked.

He'd been over the moon this morning when Daniel and he had been in the kitchen when she'd come down. Reilly hadn't gotten much sleep the night before and flushed when she thought of why she hadn't.

Daniel had kept his word on making love to her in all the places he'd said. Well, they'd missed the kitchen, but the shower and the bed had worked well for them. Better than well. She'd come so many times that she'd slept like a baby. She looked over at his mom and wondered if she knew that he'd spent the night with her. Then there was the fact that she'd said she loved him.

She hadn't meant to. It had been one thing to just realize it, but another altogether to scream it at the top of her lungs. And then the fact that he hadn't mentioned it last night or this morning made her think that he really didn't care. She turned her back to the class and looked out the window. Of course, it wasn't his fault that she had done the really stupid thing her heart had been warned about and fallen for the ass. But he could have said something, right?

Class ended an hour later. She didn't have to do much to clean up. Kasey had told her that she'd simply have to make sure that everything that needed to be saved was put into the cabinet, and the cleaning crew would take care of the rest. Benny helped her carry most of the projects over, and Mrs. Hunter drifted from one wheel to the next, seemingly at random.

"I wonder if you would have dinner with me this evening. I think Daniel is taking Benny to his house for some male bonding or some such, and it could be just you, me, and the girls." Her smile was genuine, but Reilly still didn't trust it. "We could even talk about your upcoming show."

"No, thanks." Benny was no longer going to get close to these people any more than she was. Daniel had made it perfectly clear that he was only in this for the short time, and she was going to start now breaking them of the habit of being around these people.

"I don't think you understand, Reilly. We want to get to know you better. Don't you want to get to know us?" Her voice sounded so hopeful that Reilly found herself wanting to do just that. "We're not all that bad a lot."

"I'm sure you're not, Mrs. Hunter, but as I'm sure you know, just because Daniel and I are having sex together, it doesn't really mean anything. Neither of us is looking for long ties, nor do I want my son hurt. So...." She picked up her bag and tried not to see the hurt in Benny's face. "I'll see you tomorrow if you stop by. Have a good night."

She hurried to her car and waited with the thing running for Benny to get himself situated before she left. She didn't want any of them to come to her and see what the fuck was wrong, and she certainly didn't want them to know that she had lied. She hated liars more than anything.

"I was supposed to have fun with Daniel tonight. Him and his brother Curtis was going to show me how to hit a ball." She glanced over at his stubborn face and then out the window again. "Just 'cause you don't like him doesn't mean I can't like him."

"And what happens when he's had enough of me? You going to still like him? Daniel told me that he doesn't want a

151

family, and he doesn't want to get married. I need...I'd like to have some long-term in my life. And in doing that, I have to be sure that the guy I choose is willing to commit to you as well. Not that he doesn't like you. I'm sure he does, but it's not really fair to him or us that we can't think of this as something that may lead to more."

He looked out the window, and she could see tears on his lashes. She hurt for him and wondered before he'd come to live with her if there had ever been a man in his life that had made any positive mark on his life. She doubted it. Meagen wouldn't have been able to bring anyone into the home for fear of Carver finding out, and even he wasn't all that great of a person.

"Is it because of me that he won't marry you?" She nearly jerked them off the road at his question. "It is, isn't it? I'm not ever going to be his kid, and he thinks he'd have to raise another man's bastard, and it's not worth it."

"I have no idea where you got that notion, but that certainly isn't true. You may be another man's bastard, but you don't have anything of him in you." She brushed angrily at the tears on her own cheeks. "My sister wasn't a great person, but she kept you safe. Safe for me. And any person, man or woman, that calls you that is going to have to answer to me. Understand?"

"Yes, ma'am. But he—"

"But he nothing. It's us, Benny, and no one else. Daniel is a nice man, but he has his own guidelines that he runs his life by. You and I aren't much different. Don't you have things you want, things you desire?" He nodded. "Well, so do I. And if I have to give up certain things to make them happen, then so be it. I'm sure Daniel is doing that."

He stared out the window for a long time. He didn't speak again until they pulled into the gate and pulled in the garage door. As it lowered, she got out and pressed the code to engage the electric in the fence and to disable all codes as of now. She pressed in the numbers the tumbler near the keypad had spit out for her and programmed the gate to those. They were locked in for the night.

"Reilly, did you leave the back door opened?" It was his voice that terrified her. He had spoken low, but she could hear the fear there. She shook her head and pulled out her cell. She was dialing the police even as she pressed the first numbers in the keypad. The woman that walked out of her house had her shoving Benny behind her.

"He's on the property. Go back." Before the girl could continue, she dropped to the ground. Blood blossomed on her shoulder. "Get inside, and I'll try to hold him off."

"Sure, you will." Reilly looked at Benny. "You know what to do. Go."

Reilly lifted the woman off the ground. She had no idea why she trusted her, but something in her did. Reilly watched as Benny sprinted toward the studio and paused long enough to key in the code before going inside. By the time the woman and her got there, if they got there, she knew there'd be no trace of him.

"You have to let me go. I'm only slowing you down." The girl had taken more than the bullet to her shoulder, Reilly could see now, but also one to her upper thigh. "I can hold him off for a few minutes until you get to safety."

"I'm not leaving you. Either help me or shut the fuck up.

153

I don't have the energy to argue with you right now." She looked at her phone again and realized she hadn't hit send. Doing so now could be a mistake. She knew enough about the bad guys to think this guy had to know how to get in her compound and out again without changing the code. It had been programmed to reset if someone tried more than three times to get in.

The next two shots sounded, and she felt the pain as it ripped through her upper arm. With the second shot, she felt the concrete of her driveway cut her cheek when it broke from a stray bullet. Then the glass to her kitchen window behind her shattered. She pulled the girl to the large concrete wall she'd had built in after she had the place revamped.

"You should know that I have plenty of bullets here with your name on them, Mrs. Harlequin. I certainly hope that your husband hasn't called the police. It might not go well for your kid."

She knew that he was bluffing about having Benny. She'd seen him go into the building. No one but she and Benny had the codes to the room he was supposed to go into, and when the outside lights over the door started flashing, she knew he'd made it safely.

"Who the fuck are you, and what do you want?" Reilly realized that he wasn't the man who'd been calling her, and she knew that if he had been Carver, he would have killed her the first time he shot at her. The man was reputed to be an expert shot.

"Give me what my boss wants, and I'll let you and the kid go." The voice, male and incredibly stupid if he thought she would believe him, laughed. "Of course, the bitch next to you has to die. He won't be happy that you doubled back on him."

Reilly looked at the girl. She shook her head. "He's going to kill us all, and you have to know it. And I know you don't have the backpack. I spoke to an agent yesterday that said he had it. And don't ask. I haven't the slightest clue who he is."

Think, Reilly, she thought. *He knows where you are, and the shots came from in front of you.* She looked that way. *Okay, there was a tree and several bushes, but they weren't big enough to hide Benny, much less a man.* She looked at the trajectory mark in the driveway. It had come from high up. She scanned the garage and saw a spark of something. The second pain hit her in the same arm. She knew it wasn't bad, but she saw him this time.

Now it was a game of waiting, which she knew she was no good at. She put her finger to her lips to tell the girl to be quiet and started to stand. She wasn't going to give him a big target but just give him enough that he'd stand. When he did, she didn't even think about it but fired at him before he was in a position to shoot at her. When he tumbled off the garage and into the bushes below it, she heard the sirens. Benny had done his job.

Chapter 15

"His name is Dotson, Collin Dotson, and he's a semi-big time hitman. Been looking for him for over three years. We have him on a couple of hits we thought he'd done, but he's pretty good at what he does." Alan smiled. "*Was* good at what he did, I should say. Until today, that is."

Daniel didn't give a shit. He wanted to see Reilly. Benny, too. But she was being questioned about what had happened, as well as being treated for her wounds in the hospital ER, and he couldn't get within five feet of her. He looked over at his brother when he laughed.

"What would you be doing right now if that was Kylie in there, and they wouldn't let you see her?" His brother shrugged. "Oh, so you wouldn't be worried and terrified out of your mind?"

"Nope. Because, unlike you, she's my wife, and Reilly is not. Why don't you sit down and tell me again how much you aren't in love with her and you're not going to—"

"I never said I wasn't in love with her." That shut Curtis up. And Alan looked shocked, too. "I'm very much in love with her, but I'm not going to marry her. We've agreed to play this out until we both have had enough. Then we move on. End of relationship and no sticky entanglements at the end."

Curtis looked pissed for several seconds. Then all of a sudden, he brightened. It was the smile that should have warned Daniel, but he was going to make sure that everyone understood that this thing he had with Reilly wasn't going to lead either of them down the aisle.

"So your plan is to what? Live together? Have sex whenever you want, then go your separate ways?" He shrugged again. "Sounds sort of boring. What if she gets knocked up? Or what if that kid of hers wants to start calling you 'Dad'? Will that make you run quicker in the opposite direction?"

"And what if she decides to see other people?" Alan chimed in. "Could be she doesn't feel like waiting for you to get to the unstickyness of the relationship and moves on beforehand."

Daniel felt a sudden pain in his chest. He wasn't sure how to answer those questions. Sure he'd been okay with thinking he'd be all right in ending things his way, but what if she did want to see other people? He decided that he'd simply have a talk with her about it. She was a very reasonable person. He rubbed his chest again.

"We'll end things when we end things. Not that it's any of your business, but I don't think the kid figures in this at all." Curtis cleared his throat and nodded, but Daniel had a point to make. "I don't ever want to saddle myself with kids, and I don't think that having sex with someone who has any should be a factor in the relationship at all."

"So, you're only in this for the sex." Daniel didn't like the way his brother had said that and didn't say anything. What would be the point? He knew what he wanted, and soon so would she.

"Aren't you her lawyer?" Daniel turned to the man standing behind him. He figured him for a doctor the way he was sporting a lab coat and stethoscope. "That girl they just brought in, aren't you her lawyer?"

Daniel looked at the double doors, then back at the man. "Yes, I am. Can I go and see her now? She might need me."

He didn't wait for an answer but went to the doors and through them. Daniel had to stop a nurse once to see which area O'Reilly was in but found her after a few minutes. She was sitting on the side of the bed with a gown over one side of her. The blood on her arm had him slow, but he moved forward when the nurse glared at him.

"This is an examination room, sir. You'll have to wait in the lobby with the others. There are enough people in here as it is." The nurse looked around the room before looking at O'Reilly again. "I really wish you'd let me give you something for this. It's going to hurt a great deal, and if you jerk away, it'll take a bit longer."

"I'm not going to jerk. Just put the flipping stitches in, or whatever you're going to do so I can get out of here." She looked over at him, and he could see the pain in her eyes. "What the hell are you doing here? Don't you have orphanages to close down or something?"

Daniel smiled. She was spitting mad, and he didn't care. Seeing her sitting there, he wanted more than anything to touch her. Moving forward, he was nearly to her when she shook her head at him.

"Don't." He nodded at her and pulled her mouth to his. Her soft sigh had him wanting to lay her back on the bed and take her, but he remembered only slightly that they weren't alone. Instead, he poured all he was into the kiss.

Everything else seemed to fade from them. Daniel had never been so lost in a kiss before. When she opened under his mouth, her tongue touching his, he moaned. He found he wanted to pull her from the bed and then lay her back onto it to make love. But someone poking him in the back had him lifting his head slowly.

"Mr...whoever you are, we're conducting an interview here, and you'll have to leave." Daniel didn't recognize the man standing there or anyone else in the room. He looked back at O'Reilly and smiled at the dazed look on her face. He knew just how she felt.

"I'm her attorney. And I'm staying. And until you show me some identification, she's not answering any more questions." When she started to speak, he leaned down to her ear. "Go with me on this or so help me. I'll figure out a more...sensual way to clear the room."

She blushed from the top of her head to where her neck was covered from his view. He wondered if she was pink to her nipples and decided he'd better not ask. She may have been embarrassed, but she didn't look any less pissed off.

The door opened behind him, and he heard the nurse swear. With a lift of his brow at her, she flushed as well. She muttered something about Grand Central and sat back on the stool with her mask on.

"Everyone out. Right now. I'm officially taking over this case as of this second." He glanced behind him to see his family doctor, Dana Gardner, and his mom right behind him. "Out. And if you try any of your 'agent has rules' shit, I'll call your father and give him a few insights on his son's activities of late."

"Now see here. This is a Federal case, and she murdered someone." The man looked ready to say more, but Annemarie stepped in front of him.

"Scott Davis, you get your bottom out of this room this minute, or so help me, *I'll* call your mother. The nerve. Don't you see that this woman has been shot? Twice? She's not going anywhere, and right now, she needs medical attention more than she needs you badgering her about killing a man who, from all accounts, was trying to kill her."

The agent looked ready to argue but stood up straighter before speaking. "Mrs. Hunter, you know as well as I that you have nothing on me. My mother won't believe a word you say." He held up his hand when Daniel's mom started to speak. "But you're right. She has been shot. But I will expect her full cooperation when she's stitched up."

He turned on his heel and left, taking the other men with him. None of them would look his mother in the eye because she was using that *I know what you've been up to* look on them. He'd seen it used before.

Before the door was completely closed, the nurse cleared her throat. "Can I finish now? I do have other patients to see today."

"Yes. Please, go right ahead." Daniel sat on the bed and held O'Reilly while the nurse finished up. O'Reilly never looked at him, but he wasn't concerned. He was going to protect her even if that meant from herself.

"I can't hang around here. I have to go home. Benny is there, and he is all alone." She looked at his mom and still not at him when the nurse left. "I was wondering if you could please use some of your powers for motherhood and get me out of here."

"Where is he? Benny? Where...I thought he came in with you." She shook her head. "You didn't leave him there all alone with that maniac out there, did you?"

He knew the moment the words spilled from his mouth that he'd been a little loud, and when she stood up, so did he. Daniel was sure he was going to be picking his ass up off the floor after she wiped it up with him.

"You egotistical pig headed prick. You think you have all the answers and no one but you can do a damned thing, right? Well, I got news for you, buster. I've been doing just fine on my own and will continue to do so." She ripped off the gown and tossed it on the floor as she continued. "You think I just figured out this stuff yesterday? I may not be as great at it as your mom, but I can protect us better than you can."

He couldn't hear past the buzzing in his head. She was standing before him in just her bra and pants, and his cock swelled in his pants. He had to physically reach up and close his own mouth or risk drooling on himself. Then she turned around.

"Mother fuck, what happened to you?" He forgot his

161

mother was in the room until she moved toward the two of them. "Who did that to you?"

She tried to pull away from him, but he wasn't having it. He heard his mother say something, but he was concentrating on trying to figure out what had bruised her lower back.

"I hit the ground when the first bullets began to come at me. Let me see…a bullet tearing through my chest or a cut on my lower back? Silly me, I thought getting out of the way of them was much better than wondering if I was going to hurt myself."

The bruise was about five inches wide and the entire length of her back. He was sure it was lower than he could see with her jeans on, but he didn't want to risk his life asking her to pull them off.

Dana came in as she was trying in vain to get away from Daniel. He wasn't any happier about this injury than he'd been with the bullet wounds. He ordered her into the bed and told her that he was going to run some tests. He said he was concerned about her kidneys.

"It'll only take an hour, and maybe by then the—"

"I can't stay here another hour. I have to go. I've things I have to take care of." She looked at Daniel with real fear in her eyes and lowered her voice so that only he could hear. "I have to go let him out. He won't leave until I go and get him."

Daniel looked at her. She needed to get Benny, but he couldn't let her leave injured. He told her he'd go and get him and keep him safe until she could leave. The kid wasn't all that bad, and he had enjoyed his time before with him. Daniel asked to speak to his client alone. When they left, he sat on the bed and watched her pace. She'd pulled the gown back on, much to his disappointment.

"Can you call him?" She shook her head. "Then tell me how to get him, and I'll go."

"He won't…. He likes you, but he won't…. Christ, I wish I'd stayed away." She paced some more and then sat down. When she did, he could see the pain in her eyes. She was really hurting.

"Tell me how to find him, and I'll bring him to you. I'll go—"

"You can't bring him here. Someone will…don't bring him here. Just…just leave him at the house. I'll be home soon, and we'll be out of your hair. I know you hate kids, so if you'll just tell him to stay in the house until I get there, then we'll be fine."

He was stunned by her comment that he hated kids. He didn't hate them. He just didn't want to be around them, much less hang out with them. Benny was all right. He wasn't annoying like a lot of his friends' kids were. But before he could tell her that, she started explaining how to get into their safe room.

"There's a picture on the wall to the right as you come in the door. It's a newspaper thing with a picture of me and some guy. Walk up to it and press in the guy's head. You'll hear a pop, and then the wall will move behind you." She was writing down something as she continued. "Once the wall is moved, you'll see a panel. Press this code in, then step back. The floor will open, and you can go down a flight of winding stairs."

"Will Benny be able to see me when I come down, or

163

will he be standing there waiting with a gun in his hands?" He was only half kidding. This was becoming more like something he'd read in a book and not in real life.

"No. He's not allowed to point the gun at people unless he has no choice. He can fire well, but we still need to work on when he needs to kill and when he needs to simply frighten. The stairs will lead you to a door. There is another panel there. That one is the second code. He'll be on the other side. You have to give him the safe word, or he won't go with you."

"Sierra. It's sierra, right?" She shook her head. Of course, they would change it. It would be stupid to keep using the same one over and over. She looked away before turning back.

"He's all I have in the world. Please don't let him get hurt." She wiped at the tears, and he felt his heart ache for her. "It's 'gold Oscar.'"

He repeated it twice for her, as she wouldn't let him write it down. He pulled her to him briefly and kissed her. She was quickly becoming a habit, and he wasn't all that unhappy about it.

He stepped into the hallway and asked the doctor to see her. He took his mom down to the waiting room and was surprised to see his family there. Daniel felt relief at seeing them there and asked if Royce would go with him, just in case the kid really did shoot him.

"Mom, stay with her. I want Curtis to be there too, as well as Jesse. She won't…they won't be able to bully her too much, but I'd still like for someone to be there just in case." They all agreed, and both his brothers went down the hall toward her room. The agents were waylaid by Alan, and Daniel felt better. "Mom, don't let her leave. Please. There's something…she and I have some things to talk about, and I don't want to have to hunt her down to do it."

~~~

"How much in love with her are you?" Royce asked his brother. He knew that he did, but he was wondering if his brother knew just how much the girl meant to him. For that matter, the kid as well.

"Love her? I didn't realize there was a chart to go by. How much do you love Kasey?" Daniel snorted. "I'm sure you have it all figured out."

"I love her enough to die for her. And if she were to die, I'd want to go with her." Royce did love his wife and son. More than anything in this world. "If you don't love her that much, why are you bothering with the kid?"

"He could be hurt." This time Royce snorted. "Okay, maybe not hurt, but he could be missing her. I'd hate to think of him missing her. Is that a crime?"

"Nope." Royce drove for a few more miles, not really thinking about anything. When the street came up, they went down it and weren't surprised to see police tape had been wrapped around the garage, as well as where he thought Reilly and the woman called Jeannie had been.

"What business is it of yours anyway what I do with my personal life?" Royce looked at Daniel when he asked. "I mean, last I looked, I'm over twenty-one, on my own, and have been making my own money for some time now. So I ask you again, what business is it of yours?"

"You're my brother. And I love you despite how brain

dead you can be sometimes." They parked, and Royce reached over and grabbed him by the arm before he could leave the car. "Reilly is right, you know."

"About what? About her being able to protect them better than me?" Daniel looked out the window toward the large studio. "She more than likely can. But there's something about her. Something that makes me what to be near her to protect her. I don't understand it. I mean, I've never been in love before, and to be honest, I'm not even sure I care for the feeling. It's sort of all consuming, isn't it?"

"It can be when you're trying to fight it. If you love her... *really* love her, I mean, you need to walk away now. Walk as far away from this as you can and never look back."

Daniel turned to look at him. He had the most confused look on his face that Royce wanted to laugh. Daniel shook his head and looked back at the studio.

"About five years ago, I fell in love...or so I thought. She was everything I wanted. Beautiful, sexy, and knew all the right people. She hung on my every word, and the sex was fantastic." Royce waited for him to finish, knowing that there was more to this. "She was perfect in every way. But...."

"But what, Daniel? What did she do to you?" He vaguely remembered his brother mentioning a girl. He'd been overseas on another project for the firm. When he'd returned several months later, he'd looked hurt, depressed. Worst of all, he'd looked beaten. Beaten in his heart and head. Everyone worried because Daniel assured them he was fine, but they knew that he wasn't.

"There was another man. Her husband. She'd only

wanted what…what I could give her. Not my heart, not my family; hell, Royce, she didn't even want my name. All she wanted was an opportunity to prove to her husband that she could get any man she wanted."

Royce hurt for his little brother. "Do you think that's what Reilly wants? To see if she can get you?"

"I don't know. But I do know one thing. She'll never get the chance to find out."

Daniel got out of the car and moved toward the building. Royce got out of the car and followed, wondering who the bitch was and where could he find her. When the door opened and closed behind Daniel, Royce picked up his pace. He didn't want the kid to shoot his brother…. He thought maybe if he kept on this same line, Reilly just might do it instead.

Chapter 16

Daniel tried to shake off the memory. Alisha had done a number on him back then. He'd thought that he'd never love again, much less want to keep a woman forever. He snorted to himself. Sure, and monkeys would fly. Daniel wasn't husband material. And worst yet, he was not made to be daddy dearest. He was having too much fun as a single man. Married men had curfews, had distrust, and they especially didn't have nine cars in the garage and a few more across the world they liked to play with.

He walked to the newspaper article that hung on the wall, the only thing framed on this particular wall that had her picture in it. The door behind him opened before he could press the face. Damned if he didn't laugh out loud at the man standing next to O'Reilly.

"It's the president. She didn't give them her name, just said that he was encouraging others to seek their dreams and do what they loved most. It says here that she donated a large amount of money, nearly five million, and wanted to remain anonymous." He pressed the president's face and heard a click of a mechanism move behind them. "I guess so far, so good."

The wall slid open. He watched it move without a single sound. Behind it was the panel that she'd told him would be there. He dropped to his knees and punched in the code. The thing blinked for about twenty seconds before it turned green. He almost forgot to step back. If it hadn't been for Royce, he might have tumbled down the stairs.

He watched as the stairs revealed themselves, and wondered if he was walking into a trap. He didn't really think so. She wanted Benny too badly to do that just now. *Maybe later*, he thought, when they sat down to discuss what he wanted from her. He walked down the iron stairs that emptied into a small room…so small, in fact, that Royce had to stand on the stairs to give him room. As soon as he pressed in the second code, the door opened. Benny was standing there with a gun in his hands pointed right at his chest.

"She said you weren't supposed to point that at anyone. She promised me that you'd—" The wind rushed from his lungs as Benny launched himself at him. He heard his brother inhale sharply, and wondered if Benny still had the gun in his hands.

"I was so worried about her. But when I get…is she all right?" Daniel nodded and stepped into the room when Benny pulled away. Daniel felt…sorry that he'd let him go. "She and I never used this room before, but I knew how it worked. Hello, Mr. Royce."

The room was monstrous. And from where he was

standing, Daniel figured a person could live down there in comfort for a good long time. There was even a big screen television. To his left was a kitchen with all the appliances one would ever need, including what looked to him like a freezer.

The television wasn't on, nor was the game system that was under it. The computer was set up, and from the screen that Daniel could see, the boy was doing his homework. He looked at the kid and felt a certain kinship to him. Daniel had been like that, preferring to read or do homework over watching anything on the "idiot box," his grandda had called it.

"Your mom is fine. She's been hurt, but not seriously. The doctor just wants to keep her for a little while so he can run tests. She fell again and bruised her back." Daniel didn't add that she'd killed a man, though he thought Benny might have figured that out. "I'm to take you to her."

"Hey, kid, how long can you stay down here before you run out of food?" Daniel looked at his brother and frowned. *Who cares?* he wanted to ask him. "Did your aunt design this place?"

"No, sir. We both did. She got the idea off a movie. It's a safe room. And the only thing I don't have is Internet. She was afraid that if it was here, then somebody could track us if we...why?"

Daniel wanted to know the same thing. He looked at his brother and waited. He didn't have long to wait.

"Reilly kept you safe down here, right?" Benny nodded. "And in doing so she made sure, in the event something happened to her, you could get out. Why didn't you?"

Benny flushed and looked toward the back of the room before looking at Royce again. "She said I was to wait for three days. If she didn't come, I was to get out and take the emergency bag and run."

"But you didn't want to wait, did you?" Benny dropped his head before saying in a low voice, "*no*." "I wouldn't have, either, if anything happened to someone I loved. Close it down, kid, and let's go."

Benny walked to the wall where the television was and moved it to the side. Daniel watched as a large doorway showed. He looked at his brother and asked how he knew.

"I wouldn't stay, and she wouldn't let him die down here. Plus," Royce pointed at the bag on the floor, "he was leaving, and I could see the dust on the mantle where the set was moved. He was at the door not because he was hoping to be rescued, but because he was afraid he wasn't."

Benny hadn't asked for the code, and it wasn't until they were in the car that he remembered. He decided not to tell his aunt, and he wasn't going to remind Benny that he'd not asked. They were nearly out of the drive when Benny asked where they were going. Royce answered before Daniel could.

"My house. That's where your aunt is now. Our family is there, as well as a few of our friends and your aunt. Kasey, my wife, is having everyone over for dinner." Daniel raised a brow at him. "I got a text when you were playing with the panels. Seems Mom has called a special meeting."

This couldn't be good. He looked at Benny in the rearview mirror and saw he didn't think so either. He glanced at his brother. Royce was grinning.

"What is really going on? I'm serious, Royce, if you know, you'd better tell me. Mom is calling a meeting for what?"

Royce shrugged. "She wants to see them both. And I think from what Kasey was saying last night, she wants an invite to the show. I guess your girlfriend is having a big art to-do, and mom is hoping to get to go." Royce grimaced. "It's black tie. I'm hoping that we can't get in."

"Reilly won't be at it, either. She's got about a million tickets, but she won't go. She never does." Royce turned in his seat as Daniel continued to drive. "She don't like those things. She said people want to know why she did whatever she did on each piece, and they treat her funny if she tells them she didn't know. She just wanted to do it."

"She doesn't. And have you ever been to one of her art shows?" Daniel grinned when Benny rolled his eyes. He was sure it was because he'd corrected him.

"Yes. Just one. It was boring, and I had to wear a tie. Nobody knew who Reilly was, though. She just walked around, holding my hand like she was drowning and I was her savior or something." He shifted on his seat and looked back at him in the mirror. "She told her agent that she would rather have her fingernails ripped off one at a time than to go again."

Daniel wanted to take her. And Benny. He had no idea why she hid behind the mask, the one where everyone thought she was an old man and decided to ask her when he saw her again. She was doing really well — very, very well as a matter of fact — and she should be out where people could praise her work.

172

"I think she just needs the right man taking her. Maybe if all of us was there with her, she'd be...I don't know, maybe she'd not squeeze your hand so tight." Daniel winked at Benny. "And if you help me convince her to go, then maybe I'll make sure that it's worth your while to wear a tie for her."

He snorted. Daniel was pretty sure he got that nice habit from his aunt and laughed. He looked over at Royce when they got to his house, and he was looking at him strangely. Daniel wasn't going to ask him what. He knew it had something to do with the conversation they'd been having earlier.

They pulled in the gated drive and up to the house. It looked to Daniel like everyone was there, including his mom. They got out, and Benny didn't move from the side of the car. He held the handle, and Daniel went to him and kneeled before him.

"I don't like people." Daniel could hear the terror in his voice. "They do things to you...make bad things happen to you."

Daniel still didn't know what had happened that day that his mother was killed and wondered if he should see if he could get Benny's help. He'd need it if this continued. His terror at strangers could cripple him in his life.

"I swear to you that while my family is very odd, they'd never hurt you. In fact, there are days when I think I have the best family in the world. My mom is a lot like your aunt. She only wants the best for everyone." Daniel watched as Kasey came out of the house with her Lee standing next to her. "See that little boy? That's my nephew Lee. That's his mom Kasey, and his dad is my brother, Royce."

Lee broke free from his mom and came at them full tilt. He was just a little over two years old now, but he still didn't run as well as he walked. Lee was almost to them when his feet tripped him up, and he started to fall forward. Benny let go of the door and grabbed him before he fell on the concrete drive.

"You almost let me falled," Lee said, and then looked up at his rescuer and smiled. "You have pretty eyes. Did you get them from your mommy?"

"No, I didn't let you fall. You tripped, and I saved you. And I got my eyes from the bas…no. I got them from my… from the man who fathered me." Benny started to put him down, and Lee grabbed him around the neck. "You can walk, kid."

"I knowed that, silly. But you can carry me. What if I falled again?" Benny looked at Daniel as if to say, "Is he for real?" then put Lee on the ground.

"I'll hold your hand, and I can snatch you up if you start to fall. And 'falled' isn't a word, and neither is 'knowed.' My aunt will have a hissy fit if you mess up."

They walked up the front stairs, and Kasey stepped back as they entered the house, talking to each other. Daniel followed and stopped in front of his sister-in-law when he got to her.

"Tricky." She grinned. "How did you know it would work? And what if he hadn't't've tried to save Lee?"

"Lee is always falling now when he runs, and after a couple of band-aids…even when he doesn't *falled* he has to have a band-aid. Anyway, the fall wasn't planned, but Lee charming him was. He's a good boy. I saw how he acted at the school that day and knew the kid had a big heart." She looked into the house, and he did as well. "She's mad at you, by the way. Do you care?"

Did he? He did plan to talk to her, and she'd thrown him out of her house several times already. Did he want to end it now? Maybe it was time. He rubbed the area over his heart. He was already in love with her. What if she started making demands, or, better yet, what if the boy did? He looked over at Kasey.

"I love her, but I'm not marrying her." She nodded. "I'm not. So whatever you have planning in your head, get rid of it. I'm thinking she and I should end it now so that you all don't get any stupid ideas."

"Good," Kasey said as she walked into the house. Daniel stood there for several seconds, wondering what had just happened. Were they all against him continuing this… whatever it was with her? Or were they trying to make him think that they didn't want him to see her just so he would? He shook his head as he entered the house. He was nearly thirty years old. He was certain they wouldn't be trying stupid childhood tricks on him at his age. Confident that he had it figured out and that he was going to break it off with O'Reilly, he walked in the house.

~~~

Benny came to her and nearly made her pass out from the pain when he hugged her tightly. She'd been so worried that Daniel wouldn't remember the codes or he'd simply not go and get him. Reilly knew he really wouldn't do that, but she needed to think the worst of him right now. Especially when she'd been shanghaied there against her will.

Mrs. Hunter was tricky. She'd have to remember that next time. She'd told Reilly that she'd take her home when the doctor released her. She'd just neglected to mention that it was her son's home and not Reilly's. When the woman she wanted to strangle most in the world sat next to her, she didn't even acknowledge her.

"You can't be mad at me forever, Reilly. I have something I need to ask you, and I need you to be at least friendly with me." Reilly looked at her as Benny and the little Hunter boy wandered off. "I need something from you, too."

"No. Whatever it is, the answer is no. If you need it in different languages, I can do that, too. *Pas du tout. De ninguna manera.* Or if you prefer in Swedish, *inte en chans jävla sätt.*" Reilly felt childish the moment she closed her mouth. Before she could apologize, Mrs. Hunter spoke again.

"You're not going to frighten me off, young lady. I know for a fact that my son loves you, and you and I are going to be best friends." She looked at the man they were talking about when he stepped up to the couch where they were sitting. "Isn't that right, son? You love Reilly?"

He stared down at her. She'd seen that look before. Not on him, but on other people when she'd seen them at shows, and the price of her work was told to them. The "mother fuck what have I gotten myself into" or her personal favorite "how the hell do I get out of this" look.

"Mom, do you think I could have a word with O'Reilly? She and I have some things to talk about." His voice sounded calm, but the look in his eyes was lust, need, and a little anger. "I'll help you to the den if you need it."

"I'm fine. But whatever you have to say isn't—"

"It is." He helped her from the couch and led her to a door she'd seen Kasey go into a few times. Even the others had gone in and then out. She figured it was to use the phone in quiet. There was enough noise in this room, and the kitchen to make someone think a war was being executed.

She went with him like she had a choice. She saw Benny with the little boy, and when he stood, she shook her head. They'd be leaving soon, and she wanted him to have as much fun as he could before they did. The door opened, and she stepped in. She moved to the desk and one of the chairs in front of it to sit down. Daniel closed the door, and she heard a small click. He had locked it.

While he stood there staring at her, she looked at the room. It was a nice sized room with bookshelves and lots of books crammed on them. The desk, where she was sitting, was huge and took up most of one whole wall. She thought it was cherry, but couldn't be sure. She did know that it was old, but the computer on it didn't look out of place.

"You and I need to talk." She looked back at him when he spoke and waited for him to continue. When he didn't, she shrugged at him before speaking.

"So, you've said. Anything in particular, or just talk? I don't do that often. I like it when it's quiet, but what topic did you want to speak about?" She put her finger to her lips and pretended to think on it. "Could it be the price of pork bellies on the market or the rising costs of gasoline?" She waited for several seconds before she dropped her own boom. "Or could it have to do with your mother's comment about you loving me?"

"You said you loved me," he snarled at her. "Or was that simply telling me you loved me fucking you?"

"No," she said to him, honestly. "No, it's the first one. I love you. But I know you don't love—"

"I do love you, damn it. I don't want to, but I fucking do. But don't think you can get your claws into me. I'm not going to marry anyone. Especially no one with a bunch of kids."

She stood up then, and he advanced toward her only to stop five feet from her. "You're smarter than I'd hoped. I wanted to knock you on your ass. Would have, too, if you'd of gotten close enough."

He waited, standing there, and so did she. She knew she could get around him but didn't want to hurt either of them to do it. She wanted out of there, out of that room and house so she could go somewhere and lick her wounds. Crying was going to be a big part of it, as well.

"You've nothing else to say?" She looked at him and saw the anger. "Nothing to say about not marrying you?" She threw back her head and laughed. Even to her ears, it sounded hollow and forced.

"I wouldn't marry you if you were the last man on earth. And as I've been telling you from the start," she said as she moved to the door. "I don't want you or your family to come around again."

He grabbed her arm. There was no time for her to get away before he had his mouth over hers. She was suddenly hungry for him. Despite the pain in her lower back, she wanted to crawl all over him and eat him alive. Before she knew it, she was on the floor and flat on her back. He'd never moved his mouth from hers.

Her shirt was up and over her breast, and then his mouth was covering her. Her nipples were being suckled and nipped. She moaned when he moved to the other breast as he did the same to it. She needed him and knew with a clarity that scared her that she always would.

When he sat up, he stripped off his shirt and tossed it away. He yanked at her pants, gym pants she'd borrowed from one of the women in this house. Before she knew it, she was naked, and he was touching her again.

He didn't say a word as he settled between her thighs. She knew what he was going to do and couldn't for the life of her think of a single thought beyond wanting him to taste her. When he ran his fingers over her mound, over her thigh, then repeated the path in the opposite direction, she closed her eyes.

"Watch me. Open your eyes and watch me eat you." She did as he commanded, but couldn't seem to open them wide with the heavy feelings of need pounding at her.

When he lowered his face to her pussy, she watched. He moved as if he had all the time in the world, and she wanted to scream at him to hurry, please.

"This changes nothing, Daniel. I never want to see you again." He grinned at her before he pressed his finger deep into her. "Christ."

He teased her. Bringing her close to her climax only to back off and start again. Reilly wanted to scream out that she'd had enough, either finish her or let her go. Her legs trembled with need, the need to come, complete this. But he continued until she was sure she couldn't take it anymore.

179

Then he sat up.

His cock was free. His fist moved up and down it so quickly that she was sure he was going to come on her any second. When he let himself go and lifted her hips up to his thighs, she felt dizzy, dizzy with not just need but love. But she bit her tongue, refusing to tell him ever again.

"I will say when we're through, you understand. I decide." He reached down and pulled her up to his body as he rested on his knees. "You're mine until I say different."

She shook her head. "Never. I belong to me." When he lifted her again and impaled her onto his cock, she grabbed his shoulders. She hung on as he laid her back on the floor.

They never spoke again. She was so close to coming again that she didn't care if he came or not. Moving her hips, she tried to get him to hit her sweet spot, but all he did was stop.

"Say it. Tell me you love me, baby, and I'll let you come." She glared at him and shifted again. "No, don't. Say it."

She needed to come, needed it more than her next breath. When he shifted on her, touching her spot, she cried out. She knew the moment that he started fucking her that she'd given him what he wanted, and when her climax strangled her, nearly tore her breath from her, she clawed at him. She felt her world slip as he filled her. Felt as if nothing, never again, was going to be the same.

Chapter 17

Berto read the report three more times. Micky was dead. So was Jeannie. And now his contact in the Feds was being taken away in chains. Chains for Christ's sake. He glanced up at the screen again when he heard the news anchor say Snodgrass again.

"It is said that he has been under investigation for nearly four years, and sources are saying that he's been a known associate of some of the biggest names in crime. He is currently being put into a secret location until it can be determined what, if any, prison will be safe for him to reside in."

"None will be safe, you stupid cunt. I have men everywhere." Berto threw his glass toward the large television stand, narrowly missing the set. "She fucking makes it sound as if he's going to be living in a posh hotel and not getting the chair. Residing, my ass."

Berto looked around the room and decided that he'd

better let the lady of the place come in soon. It was beginning to look a little like a hovel that he'd told Jeannie that it was. He thought about her as he leaned against the headboard of the bed, closing his eyes.

Dead. He knew that he had planned to kill her, but it should have been his pleasure and not some stupid fuck of a cop. And why the hell was she with Dotson anyway? The man was reputed to be the best of the best. But now, ...dead. Both of them shot by a cop trying to get into the fucking Harlequin compound. And the targets weren't even there. And now, thanks to Snodgrass being caught, he couldn't even leave this place.

If he said a single word that even sounded like his name, Berto knew that he was going to have him killed. Smiling, he thought of what he'd already managed to get accomplished. The Fed was dead, anyway, just as soon as the one person he had planted in the building at the police station followed through.

Berto knew that they'd take him there first. He himself had been arrested enough to know how it worked. Station, hidey hole, then some prison that would be named later. Yes, within the next four to five hours, Snodgrass would be dead, and he'd be flying back to his own bolt hole across the ocean. It paid to have plans. He frowned at his phone when it chirped.

"Mr. Carver. It is Rogers, sir. The house is being raided as we speak. I have told them that I know nothing as to your whereabouts, but they have a warrant. What would you have me do?"

Berto closed his phone, only to open it again. Snapping

it in two, he took out the battery as well as the sim card and pocketed it. The rest he tossed in the trash can. They knew him. The motherfucking slimy bastard had given him up. Son of a bitch, he was so fucked. And the fucking Rogers had called him.

He knew enough about technology that they could trace him. Hell, he wasn't sure even now how long it would take to do so. Minutes? Seconds? He had no clue. He slid off the bed and started pacing the room.

He had to move. But where? Money he had, ways to get there very little. He thought about the fact that he was in Ohio and where in Ohio. Did they have this place on their grid yet? He would bet not. The service here was spotty at best, and even that wasn't so good. He decided that he'd stay put for now. Hell, a town this tiny, he'd probably hear about it way before the place was hit. No, here was his best bet.

He looked at the tickets that had arrived this morning. Three of them to the art show of the girl that had everything to make his prison stay a death warrant. Jeannie had done one thing right before she'd gotten herself killed, it seemed. Now he had to figure out how to get there. The small knock at his door distracted him.

"Sir, I've been sent to clean the rooms. Is this going to be a good time for you?" The maid. He vaguely remembered telling her that he was in the middle of some business deal or another and told her to come back today. Why not?

He opened the door with his gun at his back. He was sure that the Feds had no idea where he was just yet, but there was no reason to take any chances. When he saw the woman on the other side, he opened the door wider without putting his gun away.

"Sorry. You're going to be in for a surprise, I'm afraid. I've been a somewhat messy person. Business isn't going as well as I'd hoped." No shit, he thought. "If you get me on the straight here, I'll pay you nicely."

She stopped when she walked in but said nothing. He could imagine what she was thinking. Pig. And he'd been so. The place looked like he'd been living in it for a month rather than a few days since someone had been there last. But she only nodded and pulled on gloves. He had no idea why that made him mad, but instead of letting his temper get the better of him, he simply walked out of the room and out to the porch that he'd noticed the first night he'd been here.

He had to get to the showing tonight. Was there such a thing as a limo service? He knew that there was a taxi service, but he didn't want to show up in a taxi at the gallery. He found it to be less than showy. He reached for his phone and cursed a blue streak when he realized that it was now in the trashcan in his room. He'd have to take care of that soon, as well.

Stepping off the porch and onto the sidewalk, he began walking toward Main Street. He hadn't been all that impressed so far. Why anyone would think a B&B in this nothing little town could survive was beyond him. There were several buses at this end of town. Large ones that said things like HAPPY TRAVELS or BUS OF FUN. Bus of fun? He doubted that. But there were hundreds of people milling about, going in and out of what he'd first thought were houses but discovered where shops. Must be a tourist trap, he thought and looked around for means to get to the next big city. He found it in a gas station.

The pick-up truck was probably on its last legs, but the kid putting two bucks worth of gas in it must have seen a Porsche. Berto watched as he dug in his pockets for the correct amount of money to pay for what he'd just pumped.

"I'll fill her up for you if you can take me to the next town. My car isn't running right now, and I lost my cell." The kid looked up at him with intelligent eyes. Berto was startled by that.

"Zanesville or Columbus? I can't really do the latter. I have to be at work in a couple of hours, and that would make me late. But I can do Zanesville well enough." Berto didn't answer him immediately, once again taken aback by the boy. "Of course, it would also depend on how long you want to spend there."

"Not long. A Wal-Mart. Do you have one of those around here?" Berto wanted to go there to get a phone. He knew that's where his butler had picked up the few that Berto had needed. "And if you could tell me where to find a rental place for a limo and tux, I'd appreciate it."

"Sure. We have all that." The kid pulled the nozzle off the pump. "How much you willing to put into my brother's truck? When I borrowed it this morning, I walked off and forgot my wallet."

Berto believed him. The kid looked much too smart and was too good looking to drive such a piece of shit. He told him to fill it up, then walked into the station to get a bottle of water for himself and the kid and paid cash for everything.

Forty-six bucks later, he was seated in a clean but worn truck speeding down the road.

"You aren't a basket person," the kid said. "So what brings you to our little town? I'm thinking banker or investor." The kid put his hand out to Berto. "I'm Harland James. Most call me Harley."

"Carl Peterson. And no, not either of those. I'm here to do some business in Columbus but can't stand the noise. I thought the B&B would be a nice change. I have some business there tomorrow. That's the reason for the limo."

The kid nodded. "I'm going to school there, at Ohio State. I have one more year, and I'm finished up. Then off to Harvard to finish my law degree. My ma has been helping me find my own place, and that's what I've been doing today. Moving out."

Berto only nodded. What the fuck did he care? And maybe he'd have to kill the kid after all. The world did not need another lawyer to clutter up his work.

By the time he'd gotten everything taken care of, he'd begun to like the kid. He was smart and was probably going to go places. Didn't mean Berto wasn't going to kill him, but he'd found a great deal of humor in the boy. When he dropped him off at the limo/taxi, Harley stayed outside to use his phone. Berto turned when the door opened behind him and looked at the kid.

"Gotta go, Carl. Boss called, and he needs me to come in early. You all set here?" Berto looked at the man behind the counter.

Up until that moment, no one had seen them together. When the kid turned up dead later, it was Berto's plan to be well and truly gone. But now there were witnesses. There were at least a dozen or so people working in the limo place, as well as the half dozen customers in the room with him. He nodded. The kid had no idea how lucky he was. When he started forward, taking out his wallet, the kid shook his head.

"Nah, you filled up the tank. We're square. Have a nice stay." And then he was gone. Berto put his wallet away again, thinking the kid wasn't near as smart as he'd thought. Putz is what he thought of him now and thought if he came this way again, he'd show the kid how stupid he'd been.

Twenty minutes later, he was being carried in a very nice stretch back to the B&B with not only a new phone but a tux he'd bought and a laptop he'd decided he'd use instead of the phone. He figured it was harder to catch a computer looking up stuff than it would have been if he'd used his phone to call information.

Life was suddenly much better.

~~~

They let her go and get her dress and a few things, but she was still pissed. Reilly had never met a pushier demanding bunch of people in her life. She sunk down in the tub to her chin and thought about the "rules" Daniel's mother had told them last night before she left.

"You'll not sleep together with that child in the house." Daniel laughed, and Reilly had only raised her brow. "Don't you give me that look, Daniel Robert Hunter. You know as well as I do that you two aren't married, and it's not proper you sleeping with her without that benefit."

"And he's not marrying me either. So butt out." Reilly

saw the flicker of humor on the older woman's face. "You really are too much of a pain for my tastes. As for him, he's a big boy. If he wants to sleep with ninety women in this place, I'm reasonably sure you can't do too much about it. Besides, that boat has sailed. Next rule."

"Are you using protection?" No, they hadn't. Not this time, at least. Reilly didn't answer. She had no idea what Daniel looked like right then. She was having a hard enough time not blushing. "I see," was all his mother said.

"Look, Mrs. Hunter, I'm going home. Today, as a matter of fact. And after that, our families won't have to mingle again." She looked at Daniel when he growled low. "Oh, grow up. You said yourself it was just sex. So live with it. I'm going to the show tonight, and if you behave, you can go with me. Otherwise, we are finished."

She had walked up to this room where she'd spent the night with him and filled the tub. That had been about an hour ago, and she'd reheated the water twice since then. When she heard the knock at the door, she ignored it. Reilly didn't even move when the door opened, and Daniel walked in.

"You said you loved me." She didn't look up at him when he spoke. It wasn't until his shirt hit the floor. "I want us to see this to the end."

"You have. It's over." She glanced up at him when his belt landed near the tub. "What do you think you're doing?"

"I need to take a bath. And you look…yummy. Can I join you?" His pants were folded and put over the toilet. "I can wash your back."

He had nothing on under the pants. Her mouth watered,

and she felt her body respond to how hard he was. When he stepped into the tub, she scooted forward so that he could sit behind her. When she tried to turn to sit on the other side, he yanked her back to his chest and held her.

"This doesn't change a thing." He just laughed. "I mean it, Daniel. We want two different things. And I have Benny to think of. He can't handle losing another person in his young life. Let us go."

He picked up the sponge on the side of the tub. She knew it was new; she'd taken it out of the package when she'd settled in the tub. He took his time pouring scented soap on it and then began washing her arms.

"Her name was Alisha Crosby. She had the most amazing green eyes and a mouth that would—"

"And this concerns me how? I don't want to hear about your past lovers. Not now, nor forever. I want you to tell me why you won't just let me not see you again."

"I'm telling you what happened. And it's important to you because she's the one that ruined it for me and marriage." She turned to look at him and then moved to the other side. He let her go this time.

"You're telling me that a woman that I've never met, don't care about, and haven't the slightest interest in is the reason that you won't let this relationship continue to marriage." He nodded, but before he could speak, she put up her hand. "No, let me ask you something before you tell me the woes of her. Do you love me?"

"Yes. But that doesn't—"

"I'm not finished. So you love me, and I love you, but because of some...what was she after? Your money?

Married?" She knew she'd hit it when he stiffened. "Married. She was married to someone else and didn't tell you, and you gave her your heart. And now, no one else can hurt you."

She stood up, and blindly grabbed the towel to wrap around her. She stumbled out of the bathroom and into the bedroom while he was still scrambling to get out of the tub. She was pulling on sweats when he came out, swearing at her.

"You are pathetic, you know that? Some bitch who has already ruined one life has let you ruin yours as well." She pulled a sweatshirt over her still damp body. "You think you're the only one who's had his heart broken? I got news for you buster. You're far from it."

"You have no idea what you're talking about," he yelled back at her. "You don't know what she said to me and what happened when I found out."

"Oh, boohoo. How old were you? You couldn't have been more than twenty, right?" He nodded. "So you've had what...ten years to get over this? But no, you let it fester and boil over until no other woman in the world could... you know what, I don't care." She started for the door only to have him grab her from behind and press her to the door.

"She only wanted to prove to her husband that she could get a younger man. She told me that I was a boy no matter how much money or smarts I had." She felt tears burn down her cheeks. "She took my love and trampled it on the rug while her husband and I stood there and took it."

"You mean just like you're doing to mine." His sharp intake of breath made her hurt more. "Let me go."

"O'Reilly, don't you see that—?"

"No, and I've decided that I don't want to. Let me go." He did but didn't move back. "I'm going to the opening tonight, and after that, Benny and I are going to do what the FBI wants. I want you to stay away from us after that."

He nodded but didn't move. After several seconds he took her hand. "May I go with you so that I can make sure you're safe? The Feds plan isn't foolproof."

Did she want him there? Yes, with all her heart. But could her heart take it? Probably not. But she wanted to be with him once more. Before she could change her mind, she said okay, but they were finished.

Chapter 18

He waited for her at the bottom of the stairs. His family was going as well, and he couldn't convince them to stay at home. He didn't want Benny or O'Reilly to go but knew that the plan simply wouldn't work if they weren't there.

Alan had given them the plan last night. O'Reilly and Benny were to go to the gallery as had been planned, but he was going to be her date. Husband really. His family was going for support, as were his best friends Alexander and Jared. He hoped that no one got hurt.

"The limo with the rest of the family is on their way. We'll ride with the four of you to the gallery, and when we get there, you're to stick to her like glue. Benny is wearing a vest under his tux, and the kid is going to be with an officer the entire night." He glanced over at Alan. "They'll be as safe as we can make them."

"I know that. But nothing is perfect. Besides, what if he doesn't show?" He hoped that he wouldn't, but knew he'd be there. "And what kind of bulletproof stuff is O'Reilly wearing?"

"About that…her dress isn't really anything we could work with. And she said she was wearing it because she needed the extra confidence it gave her." They both looked up the stairs when they heard her clear her throat. "See what I mean."

Daniel couldn't really see anything right at the moment. The ravishing woman in front of him took up all his vision. The dress, what there was of it, was molded to her curves and dips so closely that Daniel whimpered. A small chuckle from Alan barely registered. He took a step forward. Then another.

The black…sheath was all he could think of to describe it…looked like she'd painted it on. And the plunging neckline covered little more than her nipples and breasts before it stopped at her navel. He watched her come toward him and saw her thigh-high stocking peek out at the slit on both sides and the high heels that shimmered beneath it. When she took the last step off the staircase, he twirled his finger to have her turn around and had to put his fist in his mouth to keep from whimpering again. There was nothing there but silk over her shoulders and then across her firm ass. She turned to face him again. He was going to have to keep a very close eye on her.

Alan chuckled again. "I tried to tell you. She said she was going to stop buses. And if she had to go to this thing, she was going in style."

O'Reilly reached for her wrap that he had clenched in his hand, and he walked behind her and kissed her bare neck before draping the thing over her, and watched as she walked to the door. He looked over at Alan.

"You let anything happen to her, and I'll kill you." Alan laughed, and they went out the door. She wouldn't let him guide her; she kept pulling away. When they got to the limo, he asked Alan to give them a minute.

"What do you —?" He kissed her. Daniel felt her stiffen; then, she melted to him. His cock, already stiff, jerked in his trousers as he pulled her closer. Her arms going up and over his shoulders made him groan, and he stepped forward to press her against the car.

He could have easily taken her right then. Buried himself deep inside of her and never left. Even as he trailed kisses down her neck to her breast, he knew he should stop, but when she tossed back her head and moaned, he took her nipple into his mouth. It was going to be a long, long night.

Her fingers tangling into his hair had him looking up. They had to go, he knew, but he needed one more taste of her. Kissing her again, he pulled the dress back into place and stepped back. They were both breathing hard.

"I need to speak to you when this is over. I've something to tell you." She nodded and then shook her head. "Yes, O'Reilly. Please."

She looked ready to tell him no again but nodded. "I love you, Daniel, but I can't do this any longer. After we talk, I don't want to ever see you again."

He didn't answer her but stepped back again. He opened the door for her and helped her slide in. He had to take several deep breaths before he allowed himself to close himself into the dark limo with her. Christ, he was in major trouble here.

Daniel sat across from her. He was sure if he sat next to her, he'd throw Alan out and take her on the seat. Besides, he could see her better this way. See the way her nipples were still hard and his bite mark on her breast. He shifted on the seat. Alan started to go over the plan again when Daniel thought about his conversation with his brother.

"Do you love her?" The question had startled him. When Royce asked again, Daniel shrugged. "The reason I ask is because you seem to."

"I do, but that doesn't change how I feel about marrying her. I'm not going to be trapped again in a relationship where I have no way out."

Royce had snorted as he stood up and picked up his son. "No, I guess divorce wouldn't be something you'd even consider. So why do you want her so badly that you'll keep trying to pull her in when all she wants to do is push you away? Is it because you want something you can't have?"

That had pissed him off, and he started to say so when Lee crawled from his father to him. The kid was great, and Daniel loved him with all his heart, but happily ever after didn't happen for everyone.

"I think what you and Kasey have is great. Even Curtis and Jesse have it made, but I don't think I'm the sort of guy who can hang around for the forever. I like my freedom too much. And I don't want to be a father. Things change when you have kids. Look at you. You used to have fun all the time. Now you've sold your bike and your little Porsche. Why? For love?"

"Yes," his brother said without hesitation. "Yes, and I'd

195

give it all up again and more if I had to. I love Kasey with all my heart. Did she ask me to sell off the bike or the car? Nope. I did that because the appeal of riding either without them both with me didn't hold any happiness for me. You have no idea what it means to hold your child in your arms, to wake up to your wife every morning, and know that she'll be there for you when you go to bed."

He didn't. He'd had thoughts of waking up next to O'Reilly, but they had yet to do that on any sort of regular basis. Did he want that? Did he want to see her grow large with their baby? Yes, he had thought it would be nice to see a baby of his own. But long term...he didn't know the answer to that either anymore.

"Royce, what if I told you I'm terrified? What if I said to you that the thought of marriage to O'Reilly doesn't scare me, but the thought of making her...keeping her happy does?" He didn't look at Royce but continued looking at his brother's son. "What if I told you the thought of leaving her makes me almost as terrified as staying with her?"

Royce stood and took Lee from him. "Then I'd say you've made your own decision. Stay away from her, Daniel. She deserves more than a man who can't let go of the past any more than he can embrace the future."

He looked over at her when the door was opened, and Alan stepped out. He reached for her when she started out and held her hands in his.

"I'm sorry. I'm more sorry than I can ever be." She looked away, and he could see her eyes fill. "I've been an ass, and I know it now. Will you marry me, O'Reilly? Will you make me a better man and marry me?"

She looked at him with her mouth opened, and he reached over and closed it. She glared at him before she turned away again. He knew she was pissed about what he hadn't the slightest idea.

"You do this now. You do this right before I have to go inside that building and face hundreds of people with this question on my mind and a mad man trying to kill me. Are you fucking insane? No, don't answer that. You are." She reached for the driver's hand as she slid out. "Yes, I'll marry you. But don't think I'm going to go easy, and I'm certainly not going to put up with your crap."

She got out, and he could see her standing there waiting on him. He sat there for several seconds before he threw back his head and laughed. No, he thought she wasn't going to go easy, and he was completely all right with that. He got out of the limo and pulled her into his arms.

"O'Reilly Harlequin, I love you very much." He took her mouth and bent her over his arms in a kiss that had her nearly falling out of her dress. When he stood them both back up, he could see the flashes of cameras going off as well as people applauding behind him. "And I don't plan to make it easy for you either."

They entered the gallery together. He hadn't realized how big this thing was going to be until he looked around. Daniel knew she was famous, but the hundreds of people here were a surprise.

"They don't know me. That's why they came to see if they can figure out who the potter Harlequin is. They won't think it's me...maybe you, but not me." He looked at her and saw she was relieved by that. "But they will tonight."

197

Rachel had told him that tonight wasn't just the biggest show of O'Reilly's career, but the one where they knew the real person behind it. They'd been planning it for months now, and this was going to play well into the Feds hands, too. They were going to tell the world that she was O'Reilly Harlequin, and that she had Carver's son. He hoped to God this went as well as he'd been told it would.

The place was packed. He saw his mom there with his brothers and guided her to them. Benny was standing next to Kylie, and she was holding his hand. Daniel couldn't believe how handsome the kid looked. He took a deep breath when they were standing in front of them and looked at Benny.

"I've asked your aunt to marry me. She said yes. But I'd feel a great deal better if you told me that you'd be my son as well." He heard his mom say, "thank goodness" but kept his eyes on Benny. "I know you come as a packaged deal, and I'd be honored to have you join with us."

"I'm not her son, you know that. I'm another man's bastard." O'Reilly started to speak, but Daniel beat her to it.

"You're only a bastard if you want to be. I have no intention of treating you like anything but my son if you'll have me. Then men and women around you will answer to me if they even think that you're anything but a Hunter." Daniel put his hand out to his future. "I don't think you'll have any problems with them, but if you do, I'm pretty sure in a few years you'll be able to take them."

Royce laughed and pounded him on his back. "I guess that could be true if it were a problem. But it's not. Welcome to the family, Reilly and Benny. I hope you two have many years of happiness together."

After a few more hugs, they broke apart. He held onto O'Reilly when the drape over the large centerpiece was spotlighted. She nodded to Rachel as she took a microphone and asked for everyone's attention.

"Everyone, this is a very special night for this gallery. We not only have the most, in my opinion, beautiful pottery in the universe, but also one of the most beautiful locations in the entire world. I want to thank Hunter Corporation for allowing us to be here this evening." Rachel took out a sheet of paper and put on her glasses. "Forgive an old woman here, can't see a darned thing without them. All right then. Tonight marks the fifteenth anniversary of O. Harlequin works. O'Reilly Harlequin started throwing at the age of ten and has only improved over the years. Harlequin works can be found gracing homes and palaces all over the world. Tonight we're going to be meeting the artist responsible for these works. Ladies and gentlemen, let me introduce you to the latest Harlequin masterpiece."

The purple drape was lifted up slowly. The crowd that had gathered was quiet as it was shown to them a little at a time. When the cover was completely off, it showed the most magnificent piece Daniel had ever seen.

The piece was wide at the base and had as many as six or maybe seven smaller pieces attached to it by sheer gravity. He'd seen her throw something similar, the pieces, not the whole, when he'd seen her in the studio. As it got to its full height, he could see where she'd used her artistic flair and love of nature.

Each of the smaller pieces were a different scene. The first one was of a large forest of trees with a lake. The lake continued into the next piece where there were houses, log ones with smoke curling from the tops and rows and rows of corn planted. As the lake continued on to the next piece, there was a mountain. The mountain was snowcapped, and the sky above it was dark and ominous looking. He couldn't see what was on the other pieces without walking around. Before he could, Rachel spoke again.

"This piece, as well as all the others, are for sale. But before we get to that, I have another announcement to make. Ladies and gentlemen, I take great pleasure in introducing to you for the first time. O'Reilly Harlequin, potter and artist. Reilly?"

She took a step back before he could guide her forward. When she looked at him when he stopped her from what he was sure bolting, she looked at him. Panic. Terror and every other emotion he could see were right in her eyes. Daniel kissed her quickly on the mouth.

"You can do this, honey. I'll be right here when you're finished." She was shaking her head, and he nodded. "You can do this. Go on. Meet your public."

He gave her a small push and watched with bated breath as Rachel reached for her. As soon as she was standing next to the agent and her piece, the room grew silent.

"Hello. I'm Reilly Harlequin." The room still hadn't moved, and she looked to him.

The applause started out as a single person. Then it grew. After only a few seconds, the room was thundering with it. He looked around and saw there was just as much shock on everyone else's face as there had been in hers. He stepped to her when she reached for him, and he could see the faces of everyone in the room. They loved her.

~~~

Reilly couldn't smile anymore and went into the little room she'd been told she could use. Her face hurt, and she thought maybe her feet were permanently broken. She slipped her shoes off and wiggled her toes on the soft carpet. When Daniel came around the corner, she smiled. They'd had little time to talk since they'd gotten there.

"There you are." He handed her a glass of champagne. "I just saw Rachel. She's walking around on cloud nine. She said to tell you every piece is sold, and the premier piece is in a bidding war. I didn't hear how much it was at. Are you doing okay?"

"Yes. I just needed a minute. I saw Benny with your best friend's wife, Willow. She was telling him about some puppies she has. Something about their names was funny." Daniel nodded.

"Yes. Someone else had named them, and Wills didn't want to change their names. Their names are Come Here and Damn It. They have had a couple of litters already, and It is about to drop another one. I'm supposed to get one of them when they're ready." She thought he was kidding. "No. That's their names. I'm not sure, but I think Alex's son has one and he called it I Said. Not sure, though."

When he pulled her into his arms, she went willingly. "Are you sure you still want to get married? I won't hold you to it if you'd like to change your mind."

"I do. And I never want to change my mind." He nibbled at her neck, and she let him. "How much longer do you have to hang out here? I'd like to take my future wife home and make love to her in a big bed."

"Soon. I'm bushed. I've been so stressed lately that I can't wait for this to be over." She looked up at him. "I guess he's not coming."

All night she'd been worried about Carver showing up. And now it was late enough that some of the patrons were leaving. Even the Feds had become a little lax. She wondered what they would do now and decided she'd had enough and told Daniel that she needed to speak to Rachel before they left. She left the small office to go find her.

She was only out the door for seconds when she was grabbed from behind.

"Hello, my dear. I've been looking for you. You have something that belongs to me, and I mean to kill you for it."

Chapter 19

Benny saw the man seconds before he grabbed his aunt. He couldn't hear what he said, but he didn't have any problem recognizing the gun he had pointed at her head. He turned immediately and went to find Daniel. He shoved him back into the little office before he could come out.

"He's got her. He took her right outside, and he has a gun to her head. She ain't...isn't fighting him like you told her, but he's got her." Benny took a deep breath. "I forgot what I'm supposed to do for the agents."

"Take a calming breath first. Now. Tell me where they are, and I'll go and see what I can do to save her." Daniel turned him so that Benny was in the room, and Daniel was nearer the door. "I want you to sit right here until—"

"No. I'm not going to hide again while he hurts her. Never again, do you hear me?" Benny knew he'd shouted, so he closed his eyes and counted to ten. "I'm not going to let her get hurt if I can help. You can't make me."

He supposed he could. He was the adult and soon to be his uncle if his aunt lived through this. Benny was going to make sure she did, even at the cost of giving the man whatever he wanted. When the door opened again, there stood five men, the men from the house, all of them Federal Agents.

"Mr. Hunter, Benton, we need you to come out here. We have a situation." Benny snorted at the man. *Situation?*

"Has he hurt her?" The first agent said no to Daniel's question. "Has he left the building yet?"

"No, sir. He wants his backpack and the kid." The agent nodded to the fake bag that Benny had brought with him. "He knows you're his kid too."

Benny nodded. That was the plan, after all. He walked out of the room with it on his shoulder and Daniel by his side. Benny hoped he did this right. He'd been trained for it for so…there they were.

His aunt had a bloody lip, and her dress was ripped. He reached out to grab Daniel's hand and started to let it go when the man squeezed it tight. The softly spoken "steady" was more helpful than all sorts of words he could have said.

"Ah, the family has arrived. And you're the bastard that I sired with the bitch, your mom." Benny didn't speak to the man, but he did lift his chin. That seemed to tick him off. "Don't get uppy to me, kid. I don't want you as my son any more than you do me to be your daddy dearest. Give me my bag."

"Give me my aunt." The man rubbed the gun along her cheek and then under her chin. "You let her go, and I'll give you this bag."

"Yeah, right. I know the deal. There are enough cops in this room right now that I wouldn't make it to the door. Give me the bag, and I'll take your aunt with me as insurance. Or didn't they tell you that when the Feds prepped you for this little thing?"

"I didn't need it. I know what I'm doing." Benny looked at his aunt and hoped he did. "You let her go, and these guys won't shoot you here."

"Benny, do it." He looked at Reilly. She nodded at him. "You know what you have to do. Simply do it."

He didn't think he could. She and he had discussed it and gone over it so many times that he could do it in his sleep, but that was in practice. This was real.

"I don't think I can." The man snarled at him and hit Reilly with the gun. "He's hurting you now."

"Benton Reilly Harlequin, do it now or so help me I'll ground you for a month." Benny nodded and put his hand into his pocket. "Breathe deep and don't think."

The gun in his pocket had been there the entire evening. He'd only touched it when he needed assurances, like every two minutes, but he knew that now had come the time.

The Feds moved as one. They were surrounding them completely, and even if Benny did give over the bag, the man was dead. Benny took the deep breath and pulled the gun and fired at the same moment. He closed his eyes when he heard a scream. Oh no, he'd killed her himself.

~~~

Daniel sat on the floor and didn't move. He'd been tossed there when they'd rushed O'Reilly, Carver, and Benny. He hadn't moved, simply because he wasn't sure his legs would support him. His mom sat on the floor next to him after putting her wrap on the floor.

"Did you know he was armed?" Daniel laughed and said no. "I thought not. They're holding him for questioning. Did you know that?"

"Yes, ma'am. They read him his rights and put him in the back of a car. I was told to stay away if I couldn't say anything constructive." Actually, he'd been told if he didn't shut his flap that he'd be tasered. "Have you spoken to him yet?"

"No. He's fine, Daniel. Benny shot him in the head just like she'd taught him to do." She'd taught him to do a great many things, it seemed. "Curtis is with him now. Advising him to keep his mouth shut until they charge him."

"They won't. They're just trying to scare him." Alan put out his hand. "You have to come with me. I need your help."

Daniel stood and felt the room tilt. He could see the blood. Not that it bothered him all that much, but it was still a nasty reminder of what had happened. He followed Alan out of the building, and both of them watched as the coroner's van was driving away. There wasn't much anyone could have done after Carver had half his face blown off.

"Where are you taking me?" He stopped when they were headed to the ambulance. "She's in there."

"Yes. She wants to speak to you. I told her I'd bring you to her even if I had to drag you kicking and screaming." Alan gave him a hard shove. "Go tell her you love her, and then tell her to get to the hospital so they can let her go home to you."

She was looking at him when he approached. He'd

been terrified, and now…now he was pissed. The least she could have done was tell him that they had a plan. When he stopped outside the doors, the medics there stepped away, but the police only tightened around them.

"The agents would have negotiated. We didn't want him around anymore." Before she could finish, he snapped.

"So you decided to take the law into your own hands and kill him off. Brilliant. What's next? The two of you go on the road as the Harlequin Rodeo? Shall I be your manager?"

She didn't speak but nodded to the cop standing next to him. The officer moved between the two of them, and another cop shut one of the doors. He was startled out of his anger when Royce pulled him back.

"What the hell is wrong with you? Didn't you see what just happened in there? Do you have any idea what those two have been through? Or is this simply about you?"

He jerked from his brother's hands and glared at him. "She and he planned this all along. He was fucking armed, and she knew it." The ambulance pulled away with the sirens blaring.

The slap across his face had his neck snap back. He looked at his sister-in-law and nearly snarled at her to back the fuck off. But the look in her eyes had him change his mind.

"I love you very much, but right now, I could easily shoot you myself. You moronic bastard, do you think she did this on the spur of the moment? Do you think that boy didn't know that someday this was going to happen, that either of them knew? Of course, they did. That bastard would have killed her, and everyone there knew it, including that kid."

She put her arms over her chest and glared. "And you're all pissy because she didn't consult the big bad Daniel Hunter before they made plans of their own. I'm sure that next time a man has a gun to her head, Benny will back off." She shook her head. "I doubt it, and to be honest, I hope to God he doesn't. He saved her, and here you stand whining about how you didn't know. Well, I got news for you, buster. If she takes you back now, I'll never like her again."

With that, she turned and stomped away. Daniel looked at Royce. "She's wrong, and you know it."

Royce turned back and looked at him for long moments. "Is she?"

Royce walked toward the cruiser that Benny was in. The kid was nodding at something Alan was saying to him. Then he lifted his hands up, and Alan took the cuffs off him. Finally, something was going right. When Benny was let out of the back, he shook Alan's hand and nodded again. Daniel walked toward them. Benny saw him and launched himself at Daniel.

"She's okay, they said. I can go and see her with you now. Can we go right now?" Daniel looked down at Benny and nodded. "She wasn't hurt at all. I didn't hit her at all, did I?"

"No. No, you didn't hit her. You killed the bad guy, but your aunt is just fine. Other than the busted lip and the small place on her arm, she's fine." They'd taken her to the hospital to keep the media away. No one outside the few people in the room with them, mostly Feds and family, knew just what had happened.

"I want to go and see her now, okay, Daniel?" He led

him to the waiting limo and wondered if she'd let him in now or have someone shoot him. He felt like it would be the least he deserved after what he'd done.

"She would take lessons from that man and then come home and teach them to me. She said that someday that man would find us, and she didn't want either of us to be a victim." Benny looked out the window as they rode down the highway. "She told me that choices were hard to make, and I might have to pick whether to live or die or maybe whether she would or not."

"She thought she was going to die?" Daniel's heart skipped several beats as Benny nodded. "But, I thought that she was learning to protect you both."

"No. She didn't want *me* to die. I was supposed to shoot her in the heart to get to his if that was the way it happened. See, she and I had all sorts of ways to kill him if he took her. If he had her in a car, I was to kill her. Then when the car wrecked, I was to kill him. If I shot him in the heart, she said I'd be free. I guess she'll be mad at me, huh?"

Daniel shook his head. She'd planned to die tonight. His mind didn't want to stop that loop going over and over in his mind. When the door to the limo opened, he followed Benny out and tried to think through what had really happened. They made their way to the hospital emergency entrance.

"She taught you to use the gun. I'm assuming she taught you all sorts of other things as well." Benny nodded. "Martial arts?"

"Yes. And how to use a knife, as well as a rifle. She didn't want me to be helpless if he came again. I guess she was right."

209

She'd kept him safe. The hidden room, the lessons, the gun. All of them had been there for the boy, not her. She'd already figured she was going to die, but he'd been her first and only thought. They stepped behind the closed-off area, and Benny went to her.

For the most part, she ignored him. Daniel was okay with that for now. He wanted to think. She'd never told him any of this, he'd already ascertained, because he'd have tried to talk her out of it or worse, taken the gun from Benny. Then there were her reasons. He'd only seen pictures of what her sister had looked like. These two not only had seen her, but Benny had witnessed it. And Daniel would bet his last dollar that the boy would have nightmares about it for the rest of his life.

"Are you all right?" She didn't answer him, so he asked again. Her one nod wasn't what he wanted, but for now, he'd take all he could get. "Benny, I was wondering if you could go out and find my mom. I need to speak to your aunt for a moment."

Benny left, and he got a text from his brother Curtis that he had him. Daniel put his phone away and sat on the end of the bed.

"I'd very much like it if you left," she said. "I know we agreed to be married, but I think under the circumstances, we both know it wouldn't work." He didn't speak as she continued. "I'll explain it to Benny that we were thinking too much about how we're going to make this work, and you and I decided that it's the best for everyone."

"I didn't decide anything other than I want to marry you." Her look might have been funny if things weren't so grave. "I was an ass back there because I was afraid."

"It doesn't matter anymore. I understand that you need—"

"I need you. And Benny." She looked away, and he could see the tears in her eyes. A short knock at the door before it opened was all the warning they got before a nurse and a doctor walked in.

"Mrs. Harlequin, I'm going to release you. I could put some stitches in your lip there, but I believe it will heal just as nicely on its own. The bruise on your shoulder is from something hard and should heal nicely in a few days. Other than that, I don't see any reason to keep you any longer." He put a bag on the bed and smiled. "I got what you needed from the gift shop. I hope the sizes are all right."

"I'm sure they are. Thank you." She grabbed up the bag as she stood. Before she started toward what he assumed was the bathroom, she turned back to him. "I don't want you here when I come back. I think we both know that we'd never make it, and I'm glad…." She looked away again to wipe at her cheeks. "I'm glad that we didn't make a bigger mistake by marrying."

She left, and he didn't move from the bed. If she thought it was over, she was in for a big surprise. He looked over at the doctor when he cleared his throat. "I thought the two of you were married. I had no idea that…I shouldn't have let you back here."

"We'll be getting married as soon as I can get a license. She's just a tad mad at me right now, and I plan to make it up to her when I get her alone."

"Yes, well, good luck with that." The doctor looked from

the door to him again. "She does seem to be mad at you."

Daniel didn't answer but waited for the doctor to leave. When he did, Daniel got up and locked the door so that he could get started on making her understand that they weren't over.

When she came out, she was dressed in a pair of baggy sweats and a tee-shirt. He nearly lost it when he realized that she didn't have on a bra. Daniel stood up when she sat in the only chair in the room. She stiffened when he went to her, but still didn't speak.

"I've applied for our license, by the way. I have a friend at the courthouse who is going in tomorrow to get it filed for us." He smiled when she didn't speak. "I thought maybe we'd get married at my mom's house. Curtis did, and it was a very lovely wedding. Of course, we won't have that many guests. I think less than five hundred should be enough."

That brought her head up. "Less than five...I don't even know fifty people. Besides, it's a moot point. I'm not marrying you." She pulled on the slippers that matched the pants in both bagginess as well as color.

"We'll see. Did you know that we've not used any protection? I hope we've created a child. I want Benny to have a large family so he could be happy with us." He nearly burst out laughing when she leaned back and put her hands over her chest. Then he did whimper when she removed them. Her nipples were hard and straining against the material.

"I think you should get your hearing checked. I told you several times now that I'm not marrying you. You have to see it would be a major mistake."

"No, I don't see that at all." He kneeled before her, opened her knees, and moved between them. "I do see that not marrying you would be one."

"What are you doing?" He ran his hands up her thighs and then back to her knees. "Daniel, stop that, please."

"Did you know that I love you in a tee-shirt? The first time I saw you, that's what you had on. It's my favorite way to see a woman, especially you." He moved his hands up her chest and noted that she was breathing hard. "And your nipples stiff like they are makes me want to suckle at them until you come."

She leaned back, and he lowered his head to her breast. When he nipped at her through the shirt, her hands gripped his shoulders. He moved to the other breast and nibbled on the peek as he pressed his cock against her soft folds.

"Daniel. You can't do this." Her words didn't match her body. As her legs wrapped around him, he reached the top of her pants and pulled them over her hips. When she lifted for him to remove them, he knew that while she was ready for him, he still hadn't won.

She had no panties on. He was both overwhelmed and overjoyed by that. Moving back enough to look at her wet curls, he moaned when she leaned up, pulled her shirt over her head, and dropped it to the floor near her pants.

He kissed his way down her chest to her belly button. "I've thought of this all night. Every time you walked toward me, all I could think about was licking here and seeing if you enjoyed it as much as I was going to."

He swirled his tongue into her crevice, and she arched up to him. Moving down her belly, he nipped his way to

213

where he wanted to be more than anything in the world. She was moving her body up and down until he was dizzy with need.

"I love you very much, O'Reilly, and want to spend the rest of my life showing you. Making love to you and having children with you." He kissed her mound and watched her eyes close. "Marry me, please, and let me make it up to you."

"Let me come, Daniel. Please? I need to come." She opened her legs wider, and he nearly gave in. Reaching down, he opened his pants and freed his cock. "Yes, please give it to me."

It was getting more and more difficult to concentrate and not simply enter her. He swiped his tongue over her pussy and moaned at her taste. Christ, she was soaking wet.

"Marry me. Say you'll marry me and I'll give you what you want, love. What we both want." He worried her clit with his tongue and wondered who was suffering more. "Will you marry me?"

"It won't wo…please." He took her clit into his mouth and suckled it. "Daniel, please."

"Say it. Say you'll marry me, and I'll fuck you until you can't stand." He was getting desperate and nearly on the edge. When he slid his finger into her heat, he was careful not to hit her sweet spot. "Do you want to come? Give me what I want, and I'll let you."

"Yes. Christ, yes, I'll marry you. Fuck me. Fuck me now before I hurt you." His cock slipped deep into her, and she came. It wasn't going to take him much more before he joined her, but he wanted her to come again and again.

When he pulled her out of the chair and stood up, she

held him, rode him. Before he touched the wall with her in his arms, she came again. This was going to be much faster than he'd wanted. As soon as she wrapped her legs around his hips and he moved in her, she came a third time, and this time brought him with her. Taking her mouth with his, he kept them from shouting out their release and bringing the entire hospital in with them.

Chapter 20

Reilly stood near the piece and looked at it. Something wasn't right, and she couldn't put her finger on it. She walked to the other side and looked again. What was it?

"I don't see a thing wrong with it. Let's leave it until you get back, and you can have another look when it's fresher." She looked over at Joey. "The wedding is in three hours, and you need to get a shower. Besides, I promised Daniel that you'd not get wrapped up in this thing again."

She had yesterday and had nearly missed the rehearsal dinner...like she cared right now. There was something missing. She looked back at it and then at Benny, who came in the door. She turned to get a hug and felt the baby move ever so slightly under her shirt.

No one knew yet, but her and Daniel. Well, Benny knew, but that was all. She was almost four months along and had never been happier.

"Where's the top piece?" Benny asked. She looked over at her nephew. "You know, the one that has the tree leaves on it?"

She slapped her forehead and went to the car to get

it. Damn it all to hell. She'd forgotten the most important piece. After climbing the ladder, she put it in place and then had the men put the ladder away. As soon as she nodded to Jared, he turned the valve, and water began to flow from the top. When he was satisfied that nothing was going to blow, he came to stand beside her.

"Gorgeous. I mean really gorgeous. Think I could have one put in my offices? I think for all I've done, maybe I could have a discount...sort of a family discount?" She simply smiled, not telling him his wife had already talked to her about that very thing. "And shouldn't you get moving? I'm pretty sure I read that there's this big wedding going on today, and you might be the main attraction."

They all rushed to the waiting limo. She'd wanted to drive, but Joey had insisted that they take it. Then if she ran behind again, she could change in the back, and no one would be the wiser. She was pulling on her heels when they came to a smooth stop at the Hunter mansion.

Annemarie had gone all out with this wedding planning. Reilly hadn't cared and told her so. Daniel had told her she'd regret it, and now she could see why. There were more than the prearranged less than five hundred guests she'd told Annemarie to invite.

"I know, I know, but I couldn't not invite clients. They love big affairs, and this one might be the best yet. All my sons are married off now, so maybe I'll retire completely after this and watch my grandkids all day." Reilly raised her brow, and Annemarie laughed. "Okay, that was stretching it, but I think I might go on a cruise. I deserve it."

"Yes, you do. Now, let's get this party started, so I can

get back to work." Reilly laughed at the expression on her face. "I'm kidding. I know that Daniel has planned this month-long vacation for us, so I'm going to enjoy it."

And Benny was staying behind to get to know his new relatives. She only wanted to get to know his uncle right now. They went into the pool house and waited for the signal to tell them it was time. Benny came in looking all tense.

"What's up, buddy? Don't like the tux?" He shook his head. "Then what? Is Jesse giving you a hard time again?"

Jesse had been a tormentor to Benny since they'd been coming over for family Sunday dinners. Benny was very smart, and Jesse would try to find the most obscure things to test him on. Benny had only missed one of his questions out of the hundreds that Jesse had found, and Jesse had been crowing about it since.

"No. It's about the backpack. Mr. Alan brought it with him. I don't want it anymore, but he said that I get to keep it." He dropped it on the floor between them. "It's for my education, he said."

Slowly, Reilly bent to pick up the bag and looked inside. The money was still there. They had taken the ledgers a few weeks ago, but the money looked like it hadn't been touched.

"Did he say why?" She closed the bag up and set it under her chair. "I thought the Feds were taking control of this stuff."

"He said that no one will claim the money because it's been cleaned. So clean that it's as good as new." Benny kicked the bag. "My mom died for that money, and he wants me to keep it."

She looked at him hard. "And you should. Maybe you should use it for good. Make it cleaner. You're right, your mom did die for it, but she stole it for you to have a better life. Use what you need for your education like Alan suggested, but also do something good with it for your mom. Something to remember her by."

Alex opened the door and told them five minutes. Benny looked at her and nodded. "Okay. Something for her. I like that. I'll figure it out while you're gone with Daniel. Then when you get back, you can help me decide."

The wedding march sounded, and they stood up. The Hunter brides were her bridesmaids, as was Jeannie. She smiled when she thought of the undercover agent and Alan. He'd been trying for weeks to get her to go out with them. Daniel had finally told the guy to back off until she had time to heal.

Benny took her hand and stood with her at the door. She leaned down and kissed him on the cheek, wondering when he'd gotten so tall. He grinned up at her and took the first step out of the house.

"I was wondering," he said as they moved toward Daniel and his brothers, "do you think I should keep my last name or change it to Hunter? Daniel said it was up to me."

Reilly was keeping her last name and hyphenating it with Daniel's. She'd wanted to change it, but Curtis told her to ease into the change and not make it right away. She'd also talked to him about Benny's name change.

"Curtis said you could change your middle name to Harlequin and keep the Hunter, too, if you wanted. Then you'd be Benton Harlequin Hunter." He stumbled a step. "Or not."

"I was thinking maybe I'd keep it all. Benton O'Reilly Harlequin Hunter sounds like a good lawyer name, don't you think?" She smiled at him, and then before she knew it, he was handing her off to Daniel.

Benny leaned in and whispered something to him, and then nodded and stepped back when the minster asked who was giving her away. She looked at her future husband and smiled.

"Hello, beautiful," he said with a quick kiss.

The wedding was a blur, and before she knew it, she was married. Married to the best man in the world and feeling safe for the first time in four years.

Life was good.

About the Author

Kathi Barton, the author of the bestselling series Force of Nature, lives in Nashport, Ohio, with her husband, Paul. In addition to writing full-time, Kathi likes to spend time with her eight grandkids, three children, and three children-in-law. She writes to relax and have fun.

Her muse, a cross between Jimmy Stewart and Hugh Jackman, brings them to life for her readers in a way that has them coming back time and again for more. Her favorite genre is paranormal romance, with a great deal of spice. You can visit Kathi on line and drop her an email if you'd like. She loves hearing from her fans. aaronskiss@gmail.com.

Follow Kathi on her blog: http://kathisbartonauthor.blogspot.com/